BEACH BUMS

BEACH BUMS

GAY EROTIC FICTION

EDITED BY
NEIL PLAKCY

Published in the United States by Cleis Press, Inc., 2246 Sixth Street, Berkeley, California 94710.

Printed in the United States.
Cover design: Scott Idleman/Blink
Cover photograph: Caroline von Tuempling/Getty Images
Text design: Frank Wiedemann

First Edition.
10 9 8 7 6 5 4 3 2 1

Trade paper ISBN: 978-1-57344-928-1
E-book ISBN: 978-1-57344-945-8

Contents

INTRODUCTION

There's something so sexy about a beach—and the men who hang around it. Whether it's on the ocean, a lake, or a New Zealand river, beaches mean water and sunshine and handsome guys showing off what God or genetics gave them.

Pick any beach around the world, and you're bound to find excellent eye candy. These gorgeous guys are the stuff of gay fantasy—from sleek swimmers to muscular surfers and boarders to sun-worshipping naturists. Their skins are toned golden brown and their bodies shimmer with droplets of water.

The stories in this collection showcase those beach bums. From a Massachusetts winter to a hot Oregon summer, tropical St. Maarten to Venice's Muscle Beach, sweethearts and strangers meet for love, seduction, and sex to the accompaniment of the crashing surf. Younger guys, older guys, beach volleyball players and bodybuilders—they're all hot and they're all here.

Here's hoping they inspire your own beach dreams!

Neil Plakcy

GOOSEBUMPS

H. L. Champa

Jared, you might want to get down to Sand Beach. We just had a hiker report they saw someone skinny-dipping. Better go check it out."

"Copy that. I'm on it."

I couldn't believe my ears when the call came over the radio. It was barely six in the morning, the sun still trying to make its way over the horizon. I had just come on shift and already I had to deal with some idiot swimming naked. There truly was never a dull moment at Acadia National Park. Even though it was the middle of August and we'd actually had some really hot days, the water still only topped out at fifty-five to fifty-eight degrees. We had the honor of having the beach with the coldest water in all of Maine. Lucky us. It was a fact some brave and truly stupid soul was finding out.

As I walked towards the beach, I wondered if the other guys were having fun at my expense. They knew my patrol was nowhere near the beach, but here I was. If they had dragged me there as some kind of joke, I vowed to spend the rest of my day thinking of a suitable revenge. I got to the edge of the sand and my heart sank when I didn't see anyone or anything on the beach. I kept walking, just to make sure, and that was when he popped out of the water, letting out a loud yelp that echoed back quickly. Before I could do anything, the mystery swimmer was strolling calmly out of the water toward a towel and backpack I hadn't even noticed before.

He was, in fact, naked. Gloriously so, a sleeve tattoo his only adornment. His brown hair clung to his scalp and his well-muscled frame commanded all my attention. He looked like a misplaced surfer, as if someone had picked him up somewhere warm and tropical and dropped him in Maine. I knew I should be acting in my official capacity as a park ranger, but all I could do was stare at his body. My mouth was hanging open as he got closer and he shocked me even more when he spoke.

"Hi. I didn't expect to see anyone else out here."

"Obviously."

"Man, that water is fucking freezing! I don't think I can feel my feet anymore."

He wrapped his towel around his waist and I had to stop myself from groaning in disappointment. The water was still dripping off him, making him look totally edible. But I tried to focus on my job.

"Skinny-dipping is prohibited here. There are signs all over the place."

"You know, I saw that. But I figured since I was the only one here, no one would mind."

"Well, unfortunately, it doesn't really work that way. One of the hikers up on Great Head Trail saw you and reported you to the ranger service."

"Great Head Trail? You're kidding, right?"

"Nope."

"Classic."

He laughed, doubling over at the double entendre us rangers had joked about for years. I tried to keep a straight face, but I couldn't help smiling. He sighed, wiping a stray tear from the corner of his eye. He smiled as he looked me up and down.

"And you're the ranger they sent after me, huh? Does this mean I'm in some kind of trouble? I mean, it was just a little swim. No big deal, right?"

"In this park, public nudity is a ticket-worthy offense."

"So you're here to haul me in?"

"You could say that. Do you have clothes around here somewhere?"

"I do. Just give me a minute."

I turned away as he started to pull jeans out of his backpack and he laughed again.

"There's really no need to turn around now. I mean, you've already seen the show. I don't mind if you take in the encore too."

I desperately wanted to turn back around and get another look at his hot body, but I forced myself to look at the sand, pretending it was the most interesting thing in the world.

"Okay, all done. Are you going to cuff me now?"

His jovial nature made me smile, as did his laid-back approach to being caught red-handed breaking the rules.

"There's no need for that. You'll just have to come with me to the station. It's about a mile from here."

"Lead on, officer. I won't resist."

The ride back to the ranger station started in relative silence, the only noise some occasional banter over the radio from the other rangers. But my new friend couldn't stay silent for long.

"So how long have you worked here, Mr. Ranger?"

"You can call me Jared. And I've worked here about four years."

"I'm Aaron, by the way. Am I your first naked swimmer?"

I cast a glance at him; his eyes were firmly planted on me.

"In fact, you are. Surprisingly enough, most people don't skinny-dip on Sand Beach."

"Then why don't you go ahead and ask me what you really want to. It must be killing you."

"Ask what?"

He laughed, putting a hand on my shoulder. I should have pulled away from the contact, but I didn't. In fact, I loved it.

"Come on, Jared. Don't play dumb with me. You want to know what would possess a seemingly sane guy to go into that water. Nude."

I looked at him again, his crooked grin sending a shot of blood to my cock. That and the memory of him without any clothes on.

"That thought did cross my mind, Aaron."

"Well, I hate to disappoint you, but there isn't any profound reason. I just thought the water looked nice, so I went for it. It's a cute beach you have there, Jared."

"Thanks, but I can't really take credit for it. You're right. The water does *look* nice. The temperature is a whole other matter entirely."

"Yeah, I have to admit I wasn't expecting that. The scream I let out when I first got in was probably what got me busted. Oh well. Chalk it up to life experience."

I shook my head at his assessment and stopped the truck in the empty parking lot in front of the station. Everyone else was still out on their morning patrols. He followed me into the office and sat down across from my desk. I pulled out the forms

I needed to report the incident while Aaron busied himself with his cell phone.

"I'll just need to ask you a few questions, Aaron. For the form."

"Sure. Fire away, Jared."

"Are you camping here at the park or just here for the day?"

"Just the day. I just finished the Appalachian Trail a few days ago and I figured since Acadia was only 150 miles away, I had to check it out. Plus, when I travel, I always like to visit a beach. Reminds me of being at home. Well, not this one, really, but most beaches remind me of home."

"Where is home?"

Aaron smiled at me, his tongue tracing across his bottom lip. He really was so cute. My mind went back to his naked body, glistening in the morning sun, and I felt hot under the collar. I knew he must be popular on whatever beach he frequented back home.

"Is that on the form, Jared?"

"No. I was just curious."

"I like that quality in a guy. I'm from San Diego."

He slumped back in the chair and put his hands behind his head. His brown hair was starting to dry; it fell into his eyes.

"I imagine those beaches in California are a little nicer than this one."

"That is very true. But what can I say? Sand is sand. I like the way it feels between my toes."

I filled out the rest of the form and wrote out Aaron's ticket. He grabbed it from my hand and read it with a smirk. I thought it might finally get a rise out of him, but even his anger sounded calm and cool.

"Fifty bucks! Shit, if I had known that I would have bought a cheesy pair of board shorts. Saved myself thirty dollars."

"Sorry. Nothing I can do. Gotta follow the rules."

He smiled again, pulling his chair close to my desk. His stare left me feeling exposed, but I couldn't look away.

"Are you sure about that? Can't we just tear up that report and pretend this whole thing never happened?"

"I can't do that, Aaron."

"Sure you can. If you really want to, Jared."

It was my turn to laugh, but he seemed dead serious. His eyes swept down to my lips and back again, causing a flush to rise to my cheeks. I tried to defuse the situation, but my voice cracked as I spoke, undercutting my message.

"If you're planning to bribe me, it's going to cost you more than fifty dollars."

"Bribery isn't exactly what I had in mind."

He stood up from his chair and walked around the desk. I watched him with wide eyes as he tore up the ticket I had just given him, letting the pieces of paper fall onto my lap.

"Oops. I guess you'll just have to write me another one. Unless I can convince you to just let me off with a warning."

I swallowed hard, my voice once again cracking as I tried to get my words out.

"What did you have in mind, Aaron?"

"This."

He grabbed the arms of my chair and turned me to face him, dropping to his knees in front of me. I knew I should have stopped him as he unbuckled my belt, but I just couldn't. He gave me one more smile before he stuck his hand into my boxer shorts and wrapped his fist around my cock. With his free hand, he grabbed a handful of my shirt and pulled me into a kiss. His lips still tasted of salt, a product of his time in the water, and his hand started moving faster around my hard dick. I tried to moan, but his mouth swallowed all the sound. Settling my hands on his shoulders, I pushed him back, trying to get reason to return.

"Aaron, we can't do this. Right?"

"Come on, Jared. You don't really want me to stop, do you? I mean, I haven't even gotten to the good stuff yet."

I didn't get a word out before he yanked my pants and boxers down to my knees, sending the remnants of his ticket to the floor. Aaron gripped the base of my cock and ran his thumb over the slit, which had begun to ooze pre-cum in anticipation of what was about to happen. After a long pause that felt like it would never end, his hot mouth was wrapped around the head of my dick, a moan coming out of my mouth before I could stop it. I cast a glance towards the unlocked station door and briefly thought of doing the smart thing and snapping the deadbolt in place. There would be no way to explain any of this to my co-workers. All those thoughts were pushed away when I looked down at Aaron, my cock disappearing into his mouth.

My fingers wrapped in his hair, the damp strands soft as silk. My radio crackled on my desk, but I ignored it as I watched his head bob in my lap, his eyes meeting mine as he dragged his tongue up the underside of my dick and kissed the tip.

"Shit, Aaron. That feels so good."

"That's the idea, Jared."

He closed his lips around my cock again and I lifted my hips up to meet his mouth, trying to drive myself deeper into his throat. When his fingers dug into my thighs, I cried out, the slight pinch of pain making the pleasure of his mouth that much sweeter. It had been far too long since I'd been with anyone and I was afraid of coming too soon. As much as I hated to do it, I pulled Aaron off my cock, his face a mix of shock and disappointment.

"Why'd you stop me, Jared? I wasn't done with you yet."

I knew he was expected me to say something smart, something official about what a mistake we were making, but that was the last thing on my mind anymore.

"Because it's my turn, Aaron."

He stood as I slid out of my chair and onto my knees, undoing his jeans as fast as I could. He hadn't bothered to put on underwear when he dressed on the beach, and I was glad. His cock was hard and thick and I just had to take a moment to drink it in. I looked up into Aaron's eyes, lust written all over his face.

"Fuck, Jared."

Aaron hissed out his words as I took him into my mouth, easing my lips down his shaft. Much like his lips, his cock tasted of the ocean and I couldn't get enough of him. I took him as deep as I could, over and over, rocking back and forth on my knees as I sucked him off. I never dreamed that an innocent radio call would turn into something like this. He pulled at my hair, pushing me to take him deeper. I struggled a bit to keep up with the quickening pace of his thrusts, my tongue constantly moving along the bottom of his cock. I wrapped my fingers around his balls and his gasp made my cock harden even more. He dragged me to my feet, his lips back on mine before I could say a word. We got rid of the rest of our clothes. Now both of us were naked, just like he had been on the beach.

"I really want to fuck you, Jared."

He kissed my neck, tweaking my nipple between his thumb and finger.

"Wow, you really do want to get out of that ticket, don't you, Aaron?"

"I'll tell you what, if after this you still want to give me a ticket, then I'll gladly take it."

He turned me around and bent me over the desk, rubbing his hard cock against my ass.

"I don't suppose you have any condoms and stuff around here, Jared?"

My face burned red as I turned around and looked at him over my shoulder, pulling open my desk drawer where I stashed a few condoms and a tube of lube. I called it wishful thinking. I never thought I'd ever get the chance to use them.

"Wow, it really is always the quiet ones that surprise you."

He rummaged through the drawer until he found what we needed. Leaning over me, he whispered in my ear, strafing his teeth against my lobe.

"Do you do a lot of fucking here in your office, Jared?"

"No. You're the first."

"Well, there's one I haven't heard in a while."

I looked back at him and watched him sink to his knees behind me. His big hands pulled my ass cheeks apart and when his touch grazed against my pucker, I moaned, resting my head against the desk. When his lubed digit started circling my hole, I felt my knees go weak. The form I had started to fill out on Jared crinkled underneath me as I bucked back against his probing fingers, letting him open me up.

"Oh, Aaron. Fuck."

I heard him stand up behind me and looked back just in time to see him rolling the condom onto his stiff prick. He grinned at me before his face turned serious again, the head of his cock rubbing against my asshole. The tease made my cock grow harder and I wrapped my fist around it, jerking slowly as I waited for him to fuck me. When the head of his cock pushed inside me, I let out a gasp, my eyes pinched shut at the momentary bite of pain. As I relaxed, the pleasure returned and Aaron inched slowly deeper.

"God, Jared, you are so tight."

I could only groan in response, my words completely failing as he started fucking me, each stroke slow and deep. His cock filled me, stretching me to the limit with each thrust. Aaron dug his fingers into my hips, so hard I was sure I'd have impressions of his hands to remember him by. Just as I got used to his slow, plodding pace, he sped up, each thrust more forceful than the last. My desk started moving, slipping across the linoleum bit by bit as he ravaged me. His hands moved to my shoulders and he started pulling me back onto his cock, our voices growing louder in the small office. My hand moved furiously over my own dick, the ecstasy I was after getting ever closer.

"Aaron, I'm close."

I don't even know if he heard me; my words did nothing to slow him down. He continued to pound into me hard and sweat started to drip off my forehead onto the paperwork below me. I closed my eyes and in my head, I saw Aaron, walking naked onto Sand Beach. That image was all it took and I started coming all over my hand, my ass squeezing around his cock as he continued to fuck me. Aaron's steady pace devolved into a syncopated rhythm as he growled and groaned, holding onto me for dear life as he came. He gave one last weak thrust before collapsing on top of me, both of us panting to catch our breath.

We got cleaned up using the last few paper towels from the station's poorly stocked bathroom and found our clothes in the pile we'd made on the floor. I took a moment to take in his gorgeous naked body before he covered it back up. I knew the memory would have to last me. He shocked me when he leaned in and kissed me softly.

"Jared, that was amazing."

"Right back at you. It certainly wasn't how I thought I'd be spending my morning."

"So, about that ticket."

"Don't worry about it. Consider yourself warned."

"I promise if I ever get back to Sand Beach, I'll bring a bathing suit."

"If you insist, Aaron."

He picked up his backpack and headed toward the door.

"I should let you get back to work. I've got a trip to finish."

"Safe travels, Aaron."

"Try not to get eaten by a bear, Jared."

He gave me one last kiss and walked out the door, disappearing down the path to the parking lot.

A few weeks later, I got a postcard from Aaron, with a beautiful picture of a San Diego beach on the front. On the back it said: *How's the water?*

MUSCLE BEACH

Troy Storm

Hey, dork! Come spot me."

I looked around. DJ couldn't have been yelling to me. But there was nobody else around. Well, there were hundreds of people around, of course—it was Muscle Beach, after all, Venice, California. People come from all over the word just to see the place. But at that particular moment, nobody was hanging around the concrete seats overlooking the outdoor weight pen. Nobody but me.

DJ was spread out on a padded workout bench, hands on the bar parked over his magnificent chest, glaring at me. "Are you fucking coming in to give me a hand? Or are you gonna sit there with your chin down to your dick looking at me like I'm a freak of nature? I do not like being looked at like I'm a freak of nature."

"I'm coming in!" I leaped off the seat, ran toward the pen, and started to hop the low fence surrounding the workout platform.

His head waggled back and forth disgustedly. "What a dipstick. Get your ass off the wire, walk around to the front like a human being, and tell whoever's at the desk I said it's okay." He plopped his head back, eyes rolling, and lifted the bar off the stanchion. His biceps bulged, his chest bulged, his thighs bulged—and so did his skimpy workout shorts.

I raced around to the desk underneath the giant concrete barbell-shaped entrance and shot through, huffing, "DJsaiditwa sokayI'mgonnagospothim!" I tore out into the outdoor workout area.

Chest pounding, grinning like an idiot, I stood over him, watching him glower. He was perfect. A piece of living sculpture. A bronzed, magnificently shaped male. No drugs. Natural. And handsome as hell. He was thirty-two years, eight months and sixteen days old. According to Wikipedia. Nine years, two months, three days older than me.

And, finally, I was right next to him. I could hardly believe it.

With effort, he pushed the heavily weighted bar off the hooks and raised it. His eyes never left mine. He carefully lowered the bar back onto the hooks.

"You have no fucking idea what to do, do you? Dork? Dingbat? What do you call yourself?"

"I, uh, I...Daniel."

"Well, Danny my fucking dipstick boy, you've been watching me every day for, what, two, three weeks? Watching me work out, seeing how I train with the other guys, seeing how they work with me, and you've learned not one fucking thing about anything we do here." He sat up and looked me up and down. "I find that surprising, since you're in damn good shape yourself, and I don't think you got that way just by sitting on that hot concrete watching me sweat my balls in this lovely California sunshine."

"I... I'll do anything you want. Just tell me and I'll do it. Anything."

"You wanna suck my dick, Daniel?"

"Oh, god, yes! And you can fuck me till I can't stand up straight. Anything. Anything you want."

He snorted. "Well, at least we got that out of the way." He lay back down. But at least he wasn't glaring.

I was covered in sweat. *Don't let him send me away. Not now. Please. He said I looked good.* David Johanssen Messinger, Mr. Everything-There-Was-To-Be-Mr.-Of that didn't require gigantic muscles, but just required being a living work of art, tightened his perfectly proportioned hands around the bar and prepared to lift it.

"Straddle my head," he instructed, puffs of air shooting out of his pursed lips. His lush, manly lips. My mouth went totally dry. "Keep an eye," he huffed, "on my face and on my arms. If I look like... I'm gonna lose it, grab the bar."

"Grab the bar?"

"That's all I'll need. Just a little help to hang it back up. Okay. Ready. I'm going for it."

I could have passed out. The most magnificent human male specimen on the face of the earth was expecting me to save him from something that he was going to go for—was already going for! If he dropped that bar... If *I* dropped that bar!

"I'm not going to... fucking drop the damned... bar, dork... Daniel." He smirked, his mouth still puckered, his face contorted. It was a weird look. "Don't look so panicked... it's just a little help I *might* need. I'm going for more reps than I... usually can pump out... showing off for the dorky kid who's been slathering over my bod for two... maybe three... fucking weeks." He stopped talking and focused inward, concentrating.

Then he came back, refocusing as the bar with the massive

weights rose and fell rhythmically as though powered by some gigantic machine and not by a mere perfect human being. "Okay..." he confessed, puffing, "it's not... just for you. I think my left pec needs... a bit more sculpting... but I can't just lift this damn thing... with one hand, now can I?"

He was pulling my leg. Obviously that lopsided-pec thing didn't make sense. Not to me, but then, half of what the guys had been doing in the weight pen for the last two and a half weeks didn't make that much sense. I used a few weights back home, but I was a rep guy, not a power lifter.

DJ pumped away. By now a couple of the other guys in the pen had noticed, and they came over.

"How many, D?"

"Thirty-five."

"No fucking way, man!"

"Going for fifty."

His face was really red by now, but the huffs of breath were as even and under control as the astonishing arms that raised and lowered the bar.

"Trying to impress my new spotter here. Say hi to the guys, kid."

I turned toward the other men. "I..." I had never been so surrounded by so much muscle mass.

"Keep your eyes on him, kid," one of the guys snapped at me, then slammed me on the shoulder as I immediately turned back to DJ. "He's just trying to throw you off," he chuckled.

"Holy shit, D! Forty-five? Is that it? You're gonna make it, man."

DJ was really working. All of a sudden the machine began to falter. All the guys moved in closer.

"I... I might need some help," I said.

"We got your back, kid." Massive amounts of perfectly

chiseled meat moved to press up against me, hands ready to grab. I couldn't believe it. I was hard as a rock and DJ was staring right up my crotch.

His eyes shifted away and then inward again.

A huge cheer went up. Arms shot out to grab the bar and take it from DJ. He lay on the bench with his eyes closed for a moment or two, his face serene, his huge chest rising and falling as the guys yelled congratulations, the excess blood flowing from his golden face. His eyes opened to check my crotch. A quick smirk, then he sat up as the guys around continued to slap him on the back and high-five him.

He grinned, basking in the adulation, shrugging nonchalantly as if it was nothing while his fellow athletes nodded proudly. They slowly drifted away, giving him thumbs up.

"Impressed?" he asked.

"I... I..." I was speechless. Why the fuck would he even care what I thought?

He stood, sucking in and expelling huge drafts of air, rolling his shoulders. "Let's go to my pad. I need to shower. You can... soap my back...or something. Got anything better to do?"

"No."

We started out, DJ strutting ahead.

"Don't worry, kid," one of the guys hit me on the rump as I passed his bench. "I hear he goes pretty easy on his new spotters."

"If there's a problem, come see me. I could use somebody straddling my face," his buddy chortled.

Outside, DJ turned and headed toward the beach. I hurried to catch up as he returned greetings to various buddies and admirers who recognized him. A couple of cute girls came up to ask for his autograph. He signed their bikinis.

Nearing the water, we turned north, toward Santa Monica.

The gay section was more subdued there. The guys just stared, some definitely checking out the new kid. *Me!* A couple raised their hands in greeting. DJ waved back.

"I just broke fifty." He yelled, pumping a perfectly proportioned arm in the air.

"You can break me anytime you want, DJ," one of the guys yelled back, his partner agreeing with a double thumbs-up.

He chuckled. "I love this beach, man. Not only is it amazing looking"—he swept his arm in a wide arc, embracing the peaceful Pacific flooding and then retreating from the white sand—"but it's got some of the hottest bods in the universe just laid out for you to roll your eyeballs over. You been having a good time, Danny?"

"Oh, jeez, yeah!"

"Not just staring at me all day and then beating your nuts raw all night, right?"

"No... not *all* night."

He smirked and grabbed me around the neck to pull me against his massive chest, knuckling my head. "Smart mouth. I may have to teach that mouth some respect."

"Oh, god, yes. Please, sir."

He pushed me away.

"You're not serious? You don't go in for that punish-me punish-me shit, do you?" He backed away, suddenly embarrassed. "I didn't...." Now it was his time to stammer. "You gotta stand up for yourself, man, don't ever let anybody pull you down." He clapped me hard on the shoulder. "Be a man, okay? Always be a man."

I nodded fiercely. "It was a joke, DJ! No. No. I'm cool."

He stared at me. After a moment he seemed mollified and we continued up the beach. "I got a couple of buddies who're into that BD stuff, SM, whatever. Creeps me out." We trudged through the warm sand at the water's edge.

"But if you really get a kick out of that shit, it's okay," he said, looking over at me and smiling. "Whatever it takes. We've all got our needs. I've got some pretty weird kinks myself. Just don't let me know about it." He rubbed his neck. "Deal?"

I wanted to photograph him doing that. His beautifully shaped hand on his beautifully shaped neck. In the warm, caressing sunlight. On a perfect beach. With the gentle waves whispering at our feet. "Deal."

And thousands of people all over the place.

"You okay?"

"Yeah."

He stopped and looked closer.

I frowned: a manly frown. "It'll never be this perfect again, will it?" My eyes stung. He had no idea what was going through my head. I wasn't even sure I...

"Nah. So hold on to it." He looked around at the cerulean sky, the soaring cumulus clouds, the distant sailboats, the squawking seagulls. "You got a camera?"

I shook my head. I had carried all my gear the first week. Then I just got tired and only took me. Seeing was enough.

"I got one at the house. We'll take pictures. That'll help."

He held his magnificent arms wide and without hesitation I buried myself in his manly hug. David Johanssen Messinger, Mr. Perfect, hugged me hard to his chest. Only a sweaty singlet, almost dry from the warm wind, was between my heart and his. His big arms squeezed as his hands slapped me solidly on the back. It seemed a waste to die at that moment. So I didn't.

"I thought you might be different." He clipped me gently under the chin, then laughed and started back up the beach. "You should have seen the look on your face when you were trying to hop the fence. Like a kid on Christmas fucking morning running toward the presents." He gave me a thumbs-up. "Thanks. I needed that."

His apartment was tiny. Somewhere between Venice and Santa Monica, not right on the beach. He stripped to shower. "I own one of those fancy jobs. On the beach. But I can make more money renting it out and staying here. This was my first. Since the nineties, man, a long fucking time ago. Keeps me grounded." He spread his arms, presenting himself. "This beauty ain't gonna last forever. Come on," he grinned, and suddenly yanked my shorts down. "Show me what you're bringing to the table."

I stripped out of my jock. He gave me an appraising look. "You are one cute guy, Danny. You must have to beat 'em off with," he eyed my crotch, "a big stick."

I blushed. Thank god I was hung. At least there was some area in which I felt halfway adequate in DJ's presence.

Until he got hard in the shower.

"Having someone soap my ass really turns me on." He blushed slightly, though it was hard to tell underneath his all-over, water-streaked, perfect tan. "You wanna soap my dick and nuts?"

I leaned in and started sucking on his tit. DJ sighed, stretching his arms up to stroke his near-bald head. "That's fucking beautiful, man." He tickled my tight balls. "I've got a talented tongue, too," he told the top of my head. "It'll be worth waiting for." I sucked harder.

In DJ's bed, I felt like I was being initiated into Valhalla. His dick was as much a work of art as the rest of him. His balls were exquisite. I tongued them and nuzzled them and gnawed on them, sending him into paroxysms of laughter.

"You're a fucking nut," he chuckled underneath me, my face in his pubes, his head at my crotch. "When are you gonna just get to sucking my dick?"

"When I get to you begging me to." I shoved my head down between his award-winning thighs, wormed my face between his butt-cheeks, and ripple-tongued his asshole. Diddled the pucker with my lips and tugged at the surrounding circle of delicate hairs with my fingernails before trailing them over the perfect rolling hills and valleys of his ass.

He shivered and shook. "Jeez, man, you are phenomenal. Most guys, most kids.... But it looks like you're not like most guys. I fucking knew it," he muttered. "I just fucking could tell." He gave an annoyed sigh. "'Bout fucking time."

I arched to drag my head back up and explore his belly button. An inny. I button-dived with my nose while rubbing my forehead in his pubes.

Oh, jeez! A volcano enveloped my midsection. He was sucking me off! The perfect pressure. The perfect suction.

"Sorry," he snickered, between setting off explosions in my groin that ricocheted all the way to my skull. "I'm more gross than you. I can't wait, man. I want meat down my gut. And a very tasty gutful it is, too," he nodded approvingly. "Not too choky, not too piddly. Just right. I might be working away here all afternoon. And into the night. If that's okay with..."

"DJ, I'm gonna blow!"

"I was kinda counting on that." He was instantly on me again, swallowing me whole.

My whole body shook. I hung onto his ass, my face buried between his legs, his big nuts knocking against my chin, his big dick throbbing against my chest. My crotch exploded, my whole ass erupted, my entire body instantly morphed into white hot cream and spiraled through my dick to coat his insides. From the tips of his perfectly shaped toes to the ends of his perfectly cropped buzz cut. Over and over the blasts came. Emulsifying me through my dick to be injected into DJ's broiling interior.

Slowly the aftershocks subsided. Oxygen found its way back into my chest. My dick was still buried in DJ's throat. His mouth was still applying pressure, his lips pressed tight against the root of my meat. I felt like I had melded into his flesh, an extension of Mr. Perfect's perfection.

We stayed meshed for a few minutes, a few hours, a couple of days. Slowly the atoms reassembled themselves into separate bodies.

I could have stayed buried between DJ's legs forever, but it was beginning to get a little hard to breathe.

"Holy cumshots." He took his time pulling his lips up the length of my dick, keeping just enough of the head in his mouth to let him enunciate. That was incredibly sexy: talking with my dick in his mouth. I started to unload again, but there was nothing left to unload. "Holy fucking cumshots," DJ snickered again, his nose nuzzling through my crotch fur. "I came, too."

He was right. Our midsections were glued together with his viscous, gooey stuff.

He laughed, lapping at my dickhead at the same time. "I fucking came from rubbing my dick between us and you blowing a load like I've never had to suck down before." With a whoop, he hopped up from the 69 and flipped around, shaking the bed like a 5.7, and ended up facing me an inch away from my face. He was beaming. He was gorgeous.

"Where the fuck did you come from? Do your folks know you're here? Where the hell have you been all my life? Can we do this, like, a lot?" His grin was insane. "I know you're just a kid and I'm practically an old guy, but I cannot believe we are so perfectly tuned, man. I have never shot my load by just rubbing up against another guy, not even a hot little stud like you, who I was sucking at the same time and all you were doing was nuzzling my nuts. We must be like a really fucking special team. You wanna move in?"

I checked my breathing and various parts of my body to be sure I hadn't morphed over to the other side. DJ's handsome mug crammed right in my face didn't exactly help me keep my head on straight. Having a staggeringly sexy godhead angel breathing hot and heavy on my eyelids and asking me...

"DJ, you don't even know me. I mean, I've hung around for a couple of weeks, but... but... we haven't even fucked, I haven't even sucked you off. Or..." My eyes dropped to his lush lips.

He pushed his mouth against mine and we tangled tongues for the next week or so.

That worked. I emerged panting into the charged air. "You want to fuck me silly?" I begged hoarsely.

"You go first," he hoarsed back, throwing his legs over his head and spreading them wide with the grace of a racehorse sailing over the finish line.

It took a while. I had to eat him out first, his asshole was so beautiful, so needing my mouth. And then his big heavy nuts were right there. Just begging.

I fucked him; then he fucked me.

We were a well-oiled love machine.

It was bliss.

A few hours later, laying naked in his bed, we finally did the bio bit. "Why me?" he asked, softly. "I know I'm this magnificent specimen of a human being, but..."

"Glen something—and guys like him. Back in the sixties, I think. I saw their pictures on the web. Ed Fury. Those guys. He did movies. Natural. No drugs, I don't think. Just hard workouts. Really good-looking. I bet I could be one of them if I worked hard enough." I shook my head. "Those guys in *300*. They don't look like, real, to me. I know there are a lot of good-looking guys in the movies these days who take off their shirts. Their clothes even. That Ryan guy who does Captain America. All those dudes on *Spartacus*. When I saw you on cable talking about how that's what you were going for, that natural look—"

"Bishop. His name is Glen Bishop. He's still around. Old dude. Got out of bodybuilding, but he's still around. He was one of my granddad's idols."

"I just decided to come out west and see if I could meet you, since you're my idol."

DJ's thumb played with my mouth. "And so for a couple of weeks you just watched your idol idle away. How long would you have waited?"

"As long as it took."

"What were you waiting for?"

"You. To notice me. To…" I bit my lip. It was hard to put into words. "To give me a shot at getting to know you. My folks think I'm crazy, but I've been pretty independent-minded from the get go. My dad admires that. My mom is terrified I'll never settle down. But, hell, I'm just," I kissed his nose, "young enough to be your kid brother. And I've always been old for my age. I've got plenty of time to find what I'm looking for. My folks thought I had lost it when I said I was coming west, but my dad said if whatever it was didn't work out they'd always be there."

"Do they know you were looking for me?"

"Yeah. They've seen you on TV."

"You think they'd like me?"

"My mom would eat you with a spoon. Not the same spoon I'm gonna eat you with, but, yeah, they'd like you. My dad would be very impressed. And not just with the way you look. You're a nice guy. I've watched the way you worked out with the other weight dudes, how they treated you, how you treated them. Right out in the open. With all of us dorks watching. You're a nice man. A good guy. As well as the most beautiful human being on the face of the earth."

DJ grinned. "Nice to be appreciated. Y'know, nobody's ever called me that before."

I snuggled closer. "They haven't been watching for what I've been watching for."

"Did you find it?"

"Yeah."

"You wanna stay?"

"Yeah."

"What? No begging? No pleading?" His grin got bigger. "No promising to suck me off until your teeth drop out?"

"Well, yeah, that, too. But basically just a manly statement of fact."

DJ's smile softened. "It might not work. Sometimes good things just don't work out."

"And sometimes they do. Besides," I grinned, "we'll have pictures."

FEBRUARY FANTASY

Miss Peach

It was earlier than I was used to getting up, but I had been dealing with some crap at work and needed to clear my head before I went into the office a few hours later. So at dawn, I found myself wandering down to the beach.

It was not the most beautiful beach in the world. It hugged the coast of Massachusetts and after several hurricanes over the past few years, it had become mostly a rocky expanse of land with a few large rocks on which to perch and watch the waves. I had been living in this little town for only a few months, house-sitting for friends who used the place as a summer house.

It was late February, so it was downright cold. I'd hustled into my parka and made my way down the road through this quiet summer town, empty and silent, with only the sound of my sneakers and the surf to add a soundtrack. I walked quickly to get my blood flowing. I jammed my hands into my jacket pockets and pulled up my hood. In minutes, I had reached the beach and found a nice big rock to sit on. I curled my feet up underneath me and snuggled into my parka.

I stared at the waves crashing and ebbing, thoroughly engrossed in the movement of nature. I began to forget about all my problems at work. I relaxed into the wind, enjoying its sting on my cheeks. The smell of the sea air lulled me into a sweet zone.

My legs were starting to fall asleep, so I stood up to wake them up. That's when I saw him, striding toward the surf in a blue wet suit. I watched as he stretched his muscles, bending to touch his toes. He had a nicely chiseled ass.

He pulled the hood of the suit over his ears and arched back once, pushing out his torso to limber up. He watched the waves. As a big one came in, he ran into the water, fluidly disappearing into the wave. I watched him swim, head bobbing above the water every few seconds. It was like watching a dancer. He seemed to be one with the ocean. No hesitation, despite the cold.

I watched him swim toward a large rock rising out of the water about a quarter-mile from shore. He climbed the rock stealthily, walked toward the far side of it, raised his hands above his head and dove into the water, out of sight of the beach.

I looked for him in the surf until I saw his head surface a few feet away from the rock. He swam back to the place where he had entered the water and body-surfed a wave to the shore. In one motion, he stood up and strode out of the surf. I sat down quickly so I wouldn't be so conspicuous, but he noticed me anyway and waved.

I gave him a shy wave back. I watched him as he stood very close to his pile of clothes at the edge of the dunes. Deftly, he pulled off his hood and I saw the shaggy mass of silver hair as he shook it out. Then he peeled off his suit to his waist and yanked on his shirt and sweater. He slid the suit off the rest of the way and briefly before he hustled into his pants, I caught a glimpse of his naked, pert ass.

I was wishing he'd turn around so I could get the full effect. But he didn't. He got dressed as fast as possible and pulled on a parka, gathering his wet suit and heading into the dunes after giving me a quick nod of acknowledgement. I nodded back.

Wow, I thought. Just under thirty myself, I wasn't usually attracted to the silver-haired set—but this man was gorgeous. What a body! I was intrigued. Did he come here every morning? I thought he might, since this especially cold morning didn't seem to faze him.

I looked at my watch. My hands were numb, even in my pockets. I was suddenly aware again of the frigidity of the air. It was time for me to head back to the house and have a quick cup of coffee before getting to work.

The yummy sight of the morning buoyed me through the day. When I got home, I made a frozen dinner and poured a glass of wine. After eating, I sank into the plush armchair in the living room. I left the blinds open and turned down the lights, enjoying the sight of the moonlight on the water and the crisp starriness of the winter sky. I drank some more wine and relaxed.

My mind turned back to the vision I had been treated to at dawn. The sky that morning was all pink and orange. The man's blue wet suit had contrasted nicely with the dawn and the gray surf. In my mind, I painted it. If I'd had my paints with me here, I would have busted them out right then. I would have loved to capture that image on canvas.

I felt a little like Walt Whitman watching the young men on the beach. I couldn't get a good sense of how old this man was—he had gray hair, but so did many people I knew who were in their thirties. His body belied any notion of age. Such a fine ass. Such a beautiful torso.

I made up my mind that I would go to the beach the next morning at dawn, just in case he was there again. I'd try to keep myself more concealed. I didn't want to appear as though I was purposely ogling him. (But, oh, I sure was.)

After a third glass of wine and a peek at the news, I sank into the king-sized bed—a luxury for me—and started fantasizing. I imagined having my own wet suit and meeting him nonchalantly and seemingly accidentally at the edge of the water. We smiled a hello and in unison dove into the waves. As he swam, I followed closely behind him, watching his head and arms moving in and out of the water.

He climbed the rock once again. I instead swam around to the backside of it in order to make my way back to the place where we'd entered the water. There, I looked up and saw him form a diving pose and plunge into the surf. I swam ahead.

Quickly, he overtook me. I was behind him again. I imagined us riding a wave to shore and getting up at the same time. I'd say a shy hello. With a sly smile, he'd return the greeting. "I saw you watching me," he'd say. He'd move closer. "I know you liked what you saw." Then he'd put his arm around my shoulder, grabbing my head and pulling me into a ferocious kiss.

I lay in the bed, thinking about us taking that kiss farther, peeling our wet suits off, tugging them over our already-hard cocks. It was cold. We pulled our clothes and parkas on before we tumbled to the rocky ground. I imagined us moving our hands along each other's bodies and to each other's members, stroking slowly, kissing all the while. I would run my fingers through his loose silver hair as we snuggled closer under our parkas.

"My car's right there," he pointed to a Volvo parked a few feet away. "It's warmer in there…"

We'd make our way—fast—to the back seat of his car and continue our encounter.

In the bed, I was fondling my balls, stroking my hardness. Before I could get too far into the fantasy, I came with gusto and, wiping off, fell asleep, thinking, "I have *got* to get myself a wet suit."

The alarm received an angry slap. I was about to reset it for my usual wakeup time, but then remembered why I was rising so early. I debated taking a shower but realized that there was probably a narrow window in which to catch the swimming guy, so I nixed the idea. I slugged down a cup of coffee and grabbed the parka. I practically ran to the beach to be sure to catch the sunrise and to get a good seat for the show.

Sure enough, not long after I had perched on my rock, out of the dunes strode my wet suit fantasy. He stretched, arching his body in ways that made me tingle. Then, as he had the day before, he walked to the water's edge and surveyed the waves. When a promising one came closer, he ran toward it and dove in. His head disappeared for a moment. I watched for it. Pop! Up it came a few feet away from the shore and he began his swim, moving rhythmically toward the huge rock off of which he would dive. Head and arms up. Head and arms under. Head and arms up...

Finally, he arrived at the rock and climbed onto it. He shook his arms and stretched a bit more. (Yummy!) Then, he walked gingerly to the backside of the rock making sure not to slip. Again, he watched the surf and waited. He dove. I sat, mesmerized, waiting for him to appear again. It seemed to take minutes and I started to panic—until: pop! Up came his head and arms, pushing him through the water back to his starting point.

The sun was up by then, but the remains of its rising were still evident in the sky, casting a soft orange hue onto the horizon while the sun's rays made the frigid water sparkle. Wet Suit Man trudged up to the dunes, reached into a bag he'd left there, and peeled his blue suit off to his hips. Speedily, he shoved a shirt and sweater on over his head. A mere glimpse, but I did get to see a beautiful view of his well-defined chest. If that wasn't enough to make me smile, he pulled his wet suit off the rest of the way, revealing his bare ass just long enough for him to yank on some pants—no underwear—and his parka. Once he'd stowed his wet suit in his bag, he disappeared into the dunes toward the parking lot.

It was freezing out there. I checked my watch. Shit. Just enough time to get home and get my work clothes on. I would have to dash without breakfast. Not the best way to greet a morning, but I had my fantasies to keep me company.

The day dragged. In moments when I could actually catch a breather, I thought of my guy from the beach. I kept picturing him shaking out his silvery hair after removing his hood, imagining being able to help him out of that suit and into the back seat of a nice warm car. I steered clear of thinking about what I would do to him. The fear of getting a boner at work was nearly as huge as that of getting one when it was my turn in school to get up and read a book report.

Over the takeout I picked up on my way home, I pondered my situation. Here I was, alone in a summer resort town, getting up at the crack of dawn to ogle some stranger who also happened to be around and happened to like a quick swim in frigid water. What the hell was going on with me? I had always been logical and here I was, daydreaming about a mysterious wet suit–bedecked man who swam in the first light of day. I knew nothing about him. What if, up close, he was kind of homely? What if he was some sort of skeevy creep? But oh, that ass. That ass got me through the day. Was I going to get up again tomorrow? Would I ever actually *talk* to the man? Or should I buy a wet suit and just happen to want to jump in the freezing February ocean first thing in the morning?

I ceased to care for a while, as I thought about him peeling off that suit. Shaking his hair free; giving me a glimpse of some serious pectorals; showing off that nearly perfect ass. I found myself with my hand once again working its magic with that vision dancing in my mind. I focused on that vision: that hair, that chest, that ass... stroking first slowly and luxuriously, then moving with *purpose*. I came like I hadn't let loose in days. That clinched it. I'd be getting up early again.

In my parka, I positioned myself so that I was more in view than I had been. I was feeling kind of bold. I waited. I watched the sun inch its way to the sky. Where was he? Was I hoping for too much? In an instant, I saw him emerge from the dunes and plunk his bag on the sand. He tucked his hair into the hood and walked almost reverently to the water's edge. He stretched. His movements were magical. I watched with relish. He stood. He watched the waves. Like a cheetah, he pounced onto the first wave he synced with.

Out he went, a few yards from shore, and swam toward the rock where he'd climb up and jump off. I'd seen this part before. And while I loved watching the dance of his body and the water, I was waiting for the good part. It came. He headed for the dunes and began the process of taking off his suit. When his sweater was on, the top of the suit was resting on his hips, and he had donned his shirt and sweater, he looked straight at me and waved. I turned crimson and waved a mortified hello. He then turned away from me and removed the suit, moving slowly to unveil his sweet cheeks. He grabbed them and glanced over his shoulder at me. Quickly he dressed.

I couldn't move. I shook my head to make sure what I was seeing was real. He stowed his wet suit in the bag and started trudging over the stones and sand toward me. I gulped. What the hell would I say? What was going on here? I was inches from sheer panic.

In seconds, he reached me, perched speechless on a rock. "Hi," he began. "I haven't seen you before and now I see you three days in a row. I thought I was the only one crazy enough to be out here in the middle of winter."

"Uh, yeah. I'm house-sitting for some friends for the winter. I started coming here before work so I can be calm when I start my day. Can I ask you something?"

He nodded.

"Why do you do that swim in such cold water? What's with that?" I asked.

"What's with you watching me? You know what I think? I think you like what you see." He smirked. "And by the way, I like the beach at dawn. I do this all year round. Swim to the rock, dive off, swim back... just a taste of ocean before I start my day. So? Why do you watch me?"

It took me a moment to find my voice. I was startled by his bluntness. I guess I was more conspicuous than I had thought. My face reddened again. "It's just a nice view, you know, the waves, the sunrise, you..." I couldn't believe I had just said that. I had blurted it out. But it wasn't like he was mincing words.

"Don't be embarrassed. I like the attention. I like the company. There aren't many of us who stay here past Labor Day. Another face is good to see. A cute one like yours is even better."

Did he just say that?!

"Well, thanks," I said. "You make an enduring picture in my mind when I'm at work. I'll admit it. I get up earlier than I need to so I can watch you swim."

He laughed and ran his hand through his silver hair. He looked somewhere between thirty-five and fifty. At that point, I didn't care. This man was sexy and had a movie-star smile. "I like that. Look," he said, pulling his parka hood up, "my car is over there. Do you want to go sit in it?"

"We could," I said, "or you could drive us down to my place."

We got in his car and drove the three seconds it took to get to the house where I was staying. I invited him in. "Coffee?"

"Sounds good. I usually just warm up by cranking the heat in the car."

I made coffee and we stood, sipping. "So," I began, "who are you? Why did I feel compelled to invite you into my home?"

"I'm Frank. I live down near the country club. And you felt compelled because you want me to fuck you."

I was dumbfounded. "Well, you're right, and you don't mince words, do you?"

He shook his head, shedding his sweater and shirt in one sweep and stepped closer to me. Entranced, I put my hand on his chest. I caressed his pecs and nipples. He came closer. I could feel his breath on my neck. His hands were on my hips, pulling me to him. He swayed our hips in circles as he kissed my neck and behind my ear. He nipped my throat. I felt him cup my ass as his lips met mine. He tugged at the buttons of my jeans. My cock strained against the zipper. In one motion, he had my hard cock in his fingers. Very lightly, he ran his finger up and down my shaft. My breathing came in small gasps. I stepped out of my pants and pushed him, kissing, toward the bed in the next room. Before long, I had him on his back on the king-sized bed. I slid his pants from him, exposing the dick I'd been fantasizing about nonstop for the past few days. It was awe-inspiring. It wasn't amazingly long but it had plenty of girth and a curve toward his stomach. Licking its head, I thought longingly of how it would feel in my ass. The curve made deep-throating tricky, but I opened my jaws and took his entire cock, making sure to hit the spot where I nearly gag and make that lovely throat-full-of-cock sound. He moaned and fucked my throat.

My hands were busy. One hand caressed his balls; the other caressed mine.

His cock was rigid. He whispered, "Let me fuck you... please."

Immediately, I slid my mouth off him and turned over, waiting. I heard him spit on himself and make it slick. At first, he teased me, pressing the head of his cock against my asshole, rubbing it and then taking it away. I groaned in desire and anticipation. I pressed against his cock. He pushed his way in.

My back arched as I felt him move deeper with a deliberately, deliciously slow groove. I grasped the pillow with both hands and screamed into it. He yanked my hair, pulled my head up, and told me, "Go ahead. Scream. It's not like there's anyone here. I want to hear you." I had never felt anything like him slamming into my ass: that was worth something *way* past screaming. He moved in a perfect wave, in and out, in and out. He reached around and grabbed my rod, his hand part of the wave. "You're going to make me come," I whispered.

"That's right," he whispered into my ear as he fucked me and stroked my cock, all in a sweet rhythm. "And I'm going to come with you."

That was it. It was too much to control. I spurted like a geyser. As I did so, I heard his cry and felt his hot jizz splashing onto my ass. I fell onto my stomach. He lay on top of me and we breathed.

After a bit, we saw the clock and had a mutual oh-shit moment: it was later than we had thought. I should have left the house twenty minutes earlier. The details of each other would have to wait. We had to get professional and ready to work.

I told him, as we got into our cars, "Well, now *that's* something to smile about today."

"Well, maybe I'll see you at the beach tomorrow. You know,

you really ought to get a wet suit." He winked and backed out of the driveway and was gone.

"Yeah," I thought, "buy a wet suit," and left for work. My boss was going to be livid at my lateness, but I had better things to think about.

SEX ON
THE BEACH

Logan Zachary

R elax, take a deep breath, and dive in." Mark, my instructor,
took his bronzed hand, touched my bare back, and guided
me deeper into the blue surf. He looked at me through his
goggles, his snorkel dangling alongside his face in the blue
waters of Baie Longue.

I bit down on the rubber mouthpiece and wondered whose
mouth this had been in before mine. Because I worked in a
hospital, infection control was a huge issue for me, even on my
first day of vacation. Had he disinfected this? Was this guy even
certified? With all of these thoughts racing through my head,
it was no wonder I couldn't get my breathing under control
enough to be able to stick my face in the water. I seemed to be
hyperventilating each time I tried to submerge my head. That
meant I was unable to see the white sandy beach protected by
the coral reef on St. Maarten.

Mark's strong arms held me secure. "If you want to be a true
beach bum, you need to learn to relax, take a deep breath, and

dive into life and relax even more. Push away all the tension, worries, and stress. This is the best place on the French side of the island to snorkel."

"But..."

"No buts, no exceptions. Relax, float, breathe, and dive in deep, with both feet."

I tripped on my flippers and plunged under the surface. Water rushed down the snorkel tube as salty brine stung my taste buds and rushed up my nostrils.

My handsome instructor dove under the surf to save me. His strong hands wrapped around my waist and helped me to my feet. One hand groped me and despite the fear of drowning, my body reacted with a fight-or-flight response. I flew.

I spit out the snorkel and coughed. I ripped off the goggles and threw them into the water. Mark dove down to grab the gear before it sunk to the sandy bottom, and I stormed back toward the hammocks and blue-and-white umbrellas that lined the beach.

I flopped down on my beach towel and watched Mark emerge from the ocean. His green trunks clung to his hips and outlined his equipment. I could feel my periscope start to rise as he tossed his head and his blond curls sprayed water over the sand like a dog. His tight ringlets sprang up as the weight of the water left. His long legs were hairy; each muscle rippled under his deeply tanned skin as he moved.

"It takes some time to master any new skill," he said.

I opened my mouth to say something and stopped. My instructor gave off a calming effect—and his body sent my senses into overdrive. It had been a long time since I'd felt desire coming from a man. I guess working out four times a week had finally paid off. My trainer made the most out of our sessions, and my body proved it.

Mark stood over me, smiling and staring into my eyes. Water ran down his body and soaked into the sand. "Mark," he said, filling in his name for me.

"Mark, I'm on vacation. I don't want to work so hard..."

My cell phone rang in my beach bag.

I rifled through it and dug it out. The hospital's phone number flashed in the window. "Jeff Parker. Yes. Yes. Can you fax it to me here at the hotel? I'll sign it." I rolled my eyes. "Not a problem. Okay. I'll check for it in ten minutes. Bye." Closing my phone as I stood up, I picked up my towel and wrapped it around my shoulders.

"You still have a half an hour left on your lesson." Mark scanned my body as he waited for my answer.

"Bank it. I know I'll use it later in the week, I just can't use it right now." I grabbed my bag and slipped my sandy feet into my sandals. As I rounded the cabana on the beach, I saw him still standing there, looking after me. Disappointment was easy to read on his face. Guilt flooded over me for a moment, and then left as soon as the stress of work and my job returned.

I signed the form and handed it back to the girl at the business center.

She smiled and said, "I'll send it as soon as I can," as she set it down on the counter by the fax machine.

I stood staring at the sheet, uncertain if I should go until I saw it sent.

Mark entered the center with my watch in his hand. "This must have slipped out of your bag."

I grabbed my bag and squeezed it. No watch. "Thanks! I'd hate to have lost that." I took it and slipped it on my arm. "Can I buy you a drink to say thank you?"

Mark smiled. "It's just part of the job. I'd do that for anyone."

He pointed at the watch.

"You've been so patient with me. Besides, I could use one, and I'd love for you to join me. We still have that thirty minutes I banked."

Mark nodded. "Sure, I could use something about now. Follow me." He led me to a quiet corner of the resort and waved at the bartender. The man nodded and busied himself in making drinks as Mark picked out a table.

His hairy bare leg rubbed against mine as we sat down. No sooner had we settled in than the bartender set two drinks down in front of us and headed back to his post. The drink was peachy pink and tasted cool, delicious, and fruity.

Before I could ask what it was, Mark said, "I hope you're having fun at the resort. I know you're a busy man, but you have to remember you're on vacation and take advantage of all we have to offer here." He pointed out the window, but stared at me. "We don't get that many good-looking professional men here. Most are out of shape and don't want to do anything except eat and sleep in this paradise."

Gentle, rolling waves washed onto the beach and couples ran in and out of the surf. One man body-surfed in the warm waves. Several other people lay in the sun working on their tans or reading. One lone jogger dodged those he met as he ran along the water's edge.

"There's certainly a lot to look at here." I stared at him. His bright blue eyes shone, his skin glowed with the sun, and his body rippled with muscles. The stirring in my swim trunks returned and as his leg brushed up against me again, I worried my erection would rip through the fabric.

"You're beautiful, too." Mark said. He took a sip of his drink and sat back in his chair, raising his arms over his head. His arm muscles bulged; the hair in his armpit was thick and dark, unlike the blond on his head. His nipples were the size of a silver dollar and perfectly shaped. The fur on his chest fanned out and thickened as it went lower and lower.

I jerked back in my seat. What were we talking about? I had gotten lost in his body.

Mark smiled. "See, that's what I mean. Relax, daydream, float. Go with it." He reached across the table and rested his hand on my arm.

My skin burned where he touched me. I pulled back, feeling my face redden. "Sunburn," I said lamely. Why did he have this effect on me? He seemed to like me and want to spend time with me. But why?

"The intensity of the sun in the islands is powerful, but there are a lot of different kinds of powers in the islands." His leg rested against mine.

This time I let it stay, trying to ignore the warmth that flowed from his body up my leg and into my groin. My penis grew thicker, longer, harder. Why was he having such an effect on me? He wasn't my type. What was my type? Did I even have a type? Work had consumed my life at home.

He reached across the table and touched my arm. "I hope we'll be able to have some more fun and get to know each other better. What do you enjoy doing for fun at home?"

I felt my face flush and wasn't able to hold his eye contact. Why was he making me feel as nervous as a schoolgirl? I looked down at the glass in my hand and traced water droplets on the outside of the drink.

"There are a few special places I'd love to show you on the island."

And then my cell phone rang.

Mark looked at me and waited.

My skin started to crawl when I saw who was calling. "I have to get this." I pulled my arm back from his grasp and found my phone. I walked out onto the beach and listened to problem after problem pour across the airwaves. I looked over my shoulder, but Mark was gone. I almost dropped the phone, but I kicked the sand and listened as the concerns droned on and on.

The next morning, I lay face down on the warm massage table and breathed deeply. Eucalyptus and the ocean brine wafted through the open window as I waited for my massage therapist to arrive. A thick cotton towel covered my bare butt; my hands and feet hung over the edge of the table.

There was a gentle knock on the door, and it opened quietly. A low husky male voice said, "Hi, it's Mark. I'll be giving you your massage today. Our massage therapist is out sick, and I volunteered when I saw your name. I hope that's okay, Jeff. I wouldn't want you to feel uncomfortable with me giving you a massage."

"I didn't know you did massage too." I felt my arousal start to grow as he clipped on a belt with a bottle of oil. His white shirt draped over his long board shorts. A deep blue Hawaiian print covered the side panels. He stepped up to the head of the table and poured oil into his palm. He rubbed his hands together, warming the liquid with the friction. His powerful hands touched my shoulders and worked down to the small of my back. Firm, wide strokes rubbed my muscles.

"Oh, I'm not a professional, I just help out when I can, but if you don't want..." he started.

I inhaled and smelled coconut—and male. "It's fine," I lied. My arousal grew and pressed into the table as he worked over my back. This so wasn't going to work. His fingers brushed over the crest of my ass, and moved the thick towel lower and lower. His touch set my skin on fire. Desire oozed out of each pore of my body. I felt a sheen of sweat break out over my body.

"I can see you work out a lot. You take great care of your body. When do you find the time?" Mark rubbed my shoulders and a drop of sweat dripped from his brow and landed on my back. "I'm sorry. It's rather warm in here."

"Make yourself comfortable," I said, feeling the tension start to flow out of my body. "I have a trainer who kills me four times a week for thirty minutes of intense workouts."

Mark stopped my massage, unbuttoned his shirt, and tossed it onto a chair.

I turned my head to see what he was doing and saw his hairy chest and thick treasure trail. His shorts had slipped down his narrow hips, revealing two tan crescent moons. He turned and walked to me and his waistband rode just above his pubic bush. A bulge stretched the front of his shorts. I felt like Sally Field: *He likes me, he really likes me!*

He took one of my arms and stroked along my wrist, over the forearm and to my elbow. He took my fingers and interlaced mine with his. He massaged my palms with his thumbs and hit spots that sent me into sensory overload.

I prayed my raging hard-on would go away before I rolled over.

Mark completed one arm and moved over to the other one. As he moved my arm, my hand brushed against his groin and his large, firm, meaty cock took my breath away. He started on my feet and worked up my legs.

I adjusted myself, aiming my hard-on straight up, which allowed my legs to relax and spread wider.

His hands slipped up my inseam and brushed along the hair on my balls. Each testicle rose and swelled under the gentle caress, the bristly hairs tickling the tender orbs. He rolled up my thigh and over my glutes. A finger glided along the crease and up to my lower back.

A drop of sweat dropped from his brow and splashed down on my back. The warm wetness surprised me as he went down my other leg and up over my ass. The towel slipped off my body and continued off the table to the floor. My butt cheeks squeezed together, as if they could recapture the lost towel. I wished the table would swallow me whole as the cool air blew across my bare backside. I hoped Mark would pick up the towel and cover me.

Mark finished my legs and as he rounded the table, his pelvis bumped the corner.

I felt the table jerk as the edge caught his drawstring and pulled on it as he moved. I turned my head to see if he was okay, as his shorts loosened and slipped down his legs.

An old, stained jock strap strained against what it held. Holes and rips revealed tan, swollen flesh and thick dark hair, along with two massive balls. One testicle hung half outside the pouch.

I swallowed hard at the sight and quickly put my head down on the table.

"Sorry," he apologized as he bent to pull them up.

The curve of his beautiful ass framed in the old elastic made my cock jump underneath me. "Not a problem."

"You don't mind if I leave them off?" He paused as he bent over.

"Make yourself comfortable," I said, as my comfort level took a nose dive.

He looked at my naked body on the table, shrugged his shoulders, and pulled up his shorts. He moved to my butt, applied more oil to his hands, and massaged each cheek. His finger kneaded and spread my ass open as he worked. He opened his hand and palmed me, making large broad strokes over my butt and up my back. With each pass his hand moved deeper into the groove. The side of his hand rode the crease, each pass lower, his fingertips brushing my balls. Finally, one hand slid over my tender opening.

My whole body jerked at the contact and a warm wave washed over me. Precum flowed out of me and was quickly absorbed into the thick cotton sheet on the table.

Over and over, he rode the wave with the side of his hand.

There was no way I'd be able to roll onto my back now. My erection strained with painful pleasure. A moan escaped from my body, and I finally gave over to the massage, allowing my body to relax and absorb all the pleasure and sensuous joy of the moment. My arms went limp, as did my toes—but not my dick.

His hand rested on one cheek and his rich voice said, "Roll over."

"I... I... can't."

"It's not a problem. It happens to all of us. We're guys, aren't we? Like we could control it if we tried."

"No."

"Maybe we should stop this massage and go back to your room? I think you'd feel more comfortable there."

Mark picked up my robe and spread it across my back, helping my arms into the sleeves. He slipped his shirt back on, then he grabbed a thick sheet and all of my things and opened the door. I knew what this meant. He wanted more than a massage. I wanted more than a massage.

It wasn't a long walk to my room, and my raging hard-on didn't shrink at all. What was I getting into? My feet sank into the hot sand as I tried to avoid eye contact with the people on the beach. I felt like everyone knew what we were doing. I fumbled to find my key card in my pocket.

My hand shook as I tried to insert it into the slot.

Mark noticed my nerves and reached for the card. As his hand touched mine, electricity shot through my body.

Mark must have felt his effect on me. He took me into his arms and held me close. He kissed me and all my nervousness left me.

I held him tight and felt my body form to his.

Mark slipped the card in and the green came on as the lock clicked open. He pushed the heavy door in, and a wave of air conditioning greeted us.

I walked over to the bed and kicked off my sandals.

"Should we start where we left off at the door or from the massage table?" Mark asked. He spread the sheet over my bed and motioned for me to lie down. "I think we should start with you face down on the bed."

I crawled onto the bed and lay face down. "It's a lot cooler in here." But my body still burned for his touch. I was always embarrassed to be naked in front of anyone—and having a hard-on didn't help.

"Take off your robe."

I loosened the belt and he removed it. I was naked, face down on my bed, and nothing had changed. My erection throbbed underneath me as the robe pulled free. How long had it been since I was with a man? I couldn't remember.

"Roll over onto your back."

"I...can't. I need a towel."

"That's why we're here. Come on, let me show you how good a massage can feel. Please." He placed his hand on my back.

My erection throbbed underneath me.

His other hand touched my shoulder and guided me over.

I followed. My cock stuck straight up and as I lay back, it slapped my belly and sprang back up.

Mark's eyes caressed my body as I lay there naked. He had

taken off his shirt and shorts, and the pouch of his ratty jock-strap swelled as he stood there. He oiled his palms and rubbed them back and forth before he started on my chest. His circles were large and firm, and my nipples rose from his touch.

"Relax."

I felt my cock start to jump up and down. It kept touching my abs and bouncing back up. It was practically waving hello to him, demanding his attention. My face burned. I wanted his touch so bad, but I hated to show him how desperate my body was.

His hands worked my neck and shoulders. He stood above my head and stretched my neck.

Tension flowed out of my body as his magic worked, but my dick didn't listen to him. I felt wetness at the tip as it brushed my belly.

He rubbed my arms and hands again, and I savored the moment. He moved down to my feet and worked up my legs. His fingertips brushed my balls again.

I felt a small pool of precum fill my belly button. I wanted him to touch me there. Everything felt so good, and I wanted more. I wanted him naked, rubbing his whole body against mine.

His hands moved up my legs, over my hips, and along the side of my cock. He circled around and around on my abs, carefully avoiding the pool and my erection. The hair on his arm tickled my tip.

My cock jumped higher and higher. The sensation grew inside me. *Touch it, touch it,* my mind screamed. *Just once, take your hand and rub it up and down my shaft and stroke me. Stroke me!*

One finger moved to the crease of my testicle and leg as he pressed down. My penis slid along his forearm. I exhaled the air that had been trapped in my lungs. How long ago had I stopped breathing?

"Did I hit a tender spot?" he asked.

I couldn't say anything. I closed my eyes and pressed my body down into the bed.

His hand touched my balls and rested there for a few seconds. Then, so slowly that I wasn't even sure it was really happening, his palm moved up to my dick. His fingers curled around the thick shaft and just held me there. Millimeter by millimeter, he slipped up my cock. As his fingers hit the tip, a gush of precum poured out and mixed with the massage oil. The pool in my belly button overflowed and ran over my hip.

His other hand freed his straining cock from the pouch on the jock. He stroked himself as he stroked me. I reached out and touched him. His body was hot and moist; my hand slipped easily over his leg and touched the back of his hand.

He removed his jock and crawled over me on the bed.

I took his erection into my hand and clamped down gently. I wanted him so much. Together we stroked each other, slowly at first, increasing as we went. My hand became wetter and wetter as my speed increased. The feeling in my balls rose and rose, and the urgency to finish drove us faster. He bent down. His lips touched mine, and mine sought his out.

As our lips met, the kiss deepened and we devoured each other. Our rhythm increased, and I couldn't hold back any longer. My cock exploded in his hand, and my grasp on his increased.

He bucked my fist and came all over me. He collapsed on me. His body lay on top of me and he kissed me again.

There was a gentle knock on the door, followed by "Excuse me, an urgent fax for Mr. Parker. I'll just slip it under the door." A swish of the paper slid under the door.

I sat bolt upright, almost knocking Mark off the bed. My sticky hand dripped across the room as I grabbed the discarded towel and wrapped it around my waist. Wiping my hand on the upper part of my leg, I dried it as much as I could before picking up the fax. The hospital logo dominated the cover sheet. "Shit!"

Mark wiped himself and slipped back into his shorts. He waited in the corner of the room as I read the papers. "Shit, I need to respond to this."

My cell phone began to vibrate in circles on the dresser. I took a deep breath and wondered if the hospital would ever be able to do anything without me.

I looked up and realized Mark had slipped out the door. Then I wondered if Mark would do anything with me again.

For the next two days, I worked in my room. Room service brought my meals as I sat on the balcony and worked. I could look out over the ocean but was unable to step foot in it. The project wrapped up around ten that night; after faxing the paperwork, my body was wound too tight to sleep.

The hospital sent a bottle of champagne and two flutes to my room to celebrate the finished project, but I felt no sense of accomplishment. I was alone, all alone, and the cold bottle did little to lift my spirits. The night breeze blew across the water. I wished I had someone to share the moment with. I thought of Mark, the wonderful massage, his naked body, and so much more. I did have someone special... and I'd thrown him away. How stupid I had been! Then I remembered what Mark had said: "Relax, take a deep breath, and dive in."

I knew I had to find him and tell him how I felt. I grabbed the bottle of bubbly and the glasses. I didn't know where to look for him, but thought I'd start at the bar. I'd just walked in the door when I heard a familiar voice offer, "How about sex on the beach?"

I stopped and turned to see Mark sitting there.

"Excuse me?" Had I heard him correctly?

He stood and handed me the cocktail: the same peachy pink drink he'd ordered me before. "Vodka, peach schnapps, orange and cranberry juice—a Sex on the Beach. I thought it was going to be a long, lonely night so I ordered two of them—but it's something I'd like to share with you."

I took a sweet sip and enjoyed the satisfying flavors.

"Would you like to walk? Or sit and drink?" Mark motioned with his hand down the beach and then pointed to the sand. "There's a great place over to there to sit and watch the surf and stars."

"I..."

"Relax, take a deep breath, and..."

I took a long drink and drained the glass. My erection throbbed in my shorts; walking would be uncomfortable. I offered my glass back to him. "More would be nice."

Mark cocked his head to the side, motioning for me to follow. "I see you brought your own."

As he turned, I watched his tight butt. In the moonlight, I could see a shadow on the sand. The form-fitting shorts were all he wore. The thin T-shirt stretched smooth against his warm skin.

My palms started to sweat at the memory of his touch, what he felt like when I touched him, and how he made me feel. "A gift from the hospital. I hoped you'd share with me."

He led me down the beach to where a blanket lay stretched out at a secluded spot. "Sit, lay down, whatever's most comfortable," Mark said. He took the bottle of champagne from me, opened it, and filled a glass to the brim.

I knelt on the thick blanket and wiped as much sand as I could off my feet. I sat down and accepted the glass. A little spilled over the edge and onto my hand.

He poured a glass for himself and lay down next to me. He leaned on one elbow and looked at me.

I stretched out and lay parallel to him, mirroring his position, and drank half of my drink. My head started to buzz from all the alcohol after only a small supper.

"I hope you're enjoying your vacation."

I took another sip.

"Sorry about the massage. Things got a little out of hand."

"Out of hand? Your fist was wrapped so tight around my cock, nothing was going to escape. I'm sorry. Work called, and I've been stuck working in my room these last two days."

"I've missed you. You didn't show up for your snorkeling lessons. I was worried that—"

My hand shot out to touch his arm, his hairy hot arm that burned my fingers as I made contact. "I'm sorry you were worried. It was all work, not you."

"Well, that's good and bad. I guess I haven't taught you much this week." Mark let his head drop back on the blanket and stare at the stars.

I pushed up onto my elbow and looked down at him, then repeated his words. "Relax, take a deep breath, and dive in."

And I did.

I tossed my glass to the sand and rolled over onto him, wrapping my legs around him. My aroused flesh rubbed against his as I cupped his head in my hands and kissed him. A gentle kiss at first. Slowly the heat grew, our lips opened, and my tongue sought out his.

His hands came up my sides and held me to him. Our mouths sealed.

I rocked my hips into his and felt his hands work down my back to the waistband. He pushed my elastic down, and I felt the night breeze blow across my bare skin—but his kisses made me forget to be worried or self-conscious.

He freed me from my shorts and I started to pull my shirt off. As I shifted to remove an arm, Mark rolled me on my back without breaking our kiss. He slipped out of his shorts and we were naked, flesh to flesh. Sweat and precum made our dicks slide along each other. The new sensation increased our intensity.

Mark kissed down my neck and lower. His teeth rolled one of my nipples and his lips sucked hard on the aroused flesh. He sucked the nipple in deeply and pinched the other one.

My fingers combed through his curls, but I wasn't able to control his movements.

He licked down my chest, over my abs. He explored my belly button, as his razor stubble brushed the tip of my cock.

I squirmed as he went lower. My hands tried to hold him back, but his mouth found my cock and swallowed me whole. As his hot tongue licked down my shaft, I held him impaled on me.

Saliva flowed over my hairy balls and ran into my crack. Mark grabbed my hips and rocked them, forcing my dick down his throat. His thumbs tapped on my balls as a finger explored my opening.

All I could do was take a deep breath, lay back, and enjoy. I could feel precum ooze out of me and mix with his juices. Hot, wet, and slippery, it added to the growing tingles and pleasure in my pelvis.

He reached over and picked up the bottle of champagne. Without breaking the seal on my cock, he popped the cork and sent a cold fizzing spray over my abs. He sucked along my cock and let the fat end pop out just like the cork. He took a long drink from the bottle and poured a glassful over my erection.

I almost screamed from the cold tingle.

He brought his full mouth down and swallowed me again. Little bubbles hit every nerve in my dick and shot through the rest of my body. He poured more over my pelvis. Bubbles exploded along my balls and filtered into my crease. A small amount pooled around the opening and sizzled.

I flexed my butt muscles and felt the coldness enter me.

Mark poured more champagne over my face; the sweet flavor burst in my mouth and ran over my cheeks.

I drank my fill and felt the alcohol and bubbles hit my brain.

He released my cock and asked, "Did you want any more champagne?"

"No," escaped from somewhere.

He brought the bottle to his mouth, drank his share, and then brought the bottleneck to my exposed ass. He tipped the bottle over and applied pressure to my hole. He gently pressed and worked my butt to relax. The rest of the bottle poured into my bowels, and my balls almost emptied. He pulled the empty bottle out, jacked his dick once, and replaced it in my ass. His hands cradled my hips as he dove into me.

One of my hands grabbed my cock as the other reached back to stroke up and down his hairy chest.

He increased his speed.

The bubbles and his thick dick stimulated my prostate and started a chain reaction. My balls rose and my cock exploded. Hot thick cream sprayed across my chest.

Mark's hand grabbed my sensitive cock and jacked it even faster as he increased his pace. He thrust into me one more time, and I felt an explosion inside and outside. He plunged in deeper and hit my prostate gland.

My dick sent another wave across my chest.

Mark moved between my legs and grabbed his dick and mine at the same time. Together, he jerked out the rest of our loads. He collapsed on top of me and kissed me deep and long. Sticky sweetness stuck our bodies together.

I lay there for a long time, enjoying the warmth and weight on my body. A shooting star streaked across the sky. I closed my eyes and made a wish. When I opened them, he looked into mine.

"We should go skinny dipping to wash off." Mark pushed himself up and reached down to grab my hand. He pulled me across the beach and we ran into the water. He dove into the surf as I flopped down into the cool, refreshing ocean.

We swam for a while, rolling and playing in the water. The salt water washed us clean and refreshed our bodies. Emerging from the surf, we dripped dry on our way back to the blanket.

Mark motioned for me to lie down.

I jumped at the chance and scooted over for him to join me.

Mark spooned my body and wrapped his arms around me on the blanket.

I fell asleep in his arms in seconds.

The next morning I ate breakfast quickly, but didn't see Mark. My snorkeling appointment wasn't until that afternoon—and I needed to know what last night meant. I rushed across the beach searching for him.

The scuba shack stood wide open, and a moment later, Mark walked around the side. He saw me coming and set down the fins he carried and walked over to meet me. He stopped a foot away.

I looked deep into his eyes as blue as the surf, his windblown hair the color of the sun. He smiled at me and stepped into my arms. His hairy legs brushed against mine as the ocean breeze blew a tropical scent over us.

"I just wanted you to know—" I started.

And the cell phone rang in my pocket.

"You'd better take that." Mark stepped back out of my arms as I dug into my pocket.

The cell phone slid along my erection as I pulled it out. The display read Hospital.

He read the display. "Guess they really can't live without you."

I turned my back to him as I brought the phone up to my ear, and then I threw it into the surf as hard as I could. A splash, and the next wave washed over it and it was gone. I faced him and stepped into his stunned arms. I pulled him close as my mouth sought out his. We kissed deep and hard until our lungs burned and we needed to come up for a breath.

"Maybe I finally learned your lesson. I like this life so much better than what I have at home. No stress, no worry, no responsibility."

"How will you survive without stress?"

"I'll do what you taught me. Breathe deep and relax." I took his head into my hands and pulled him almost to my mouth, took a deep breath, and dove in, deep.

COCK ROCK

David Holly

I was getting closer and closer to orgasm. Riding Vance's fiery ass in the filtered sunlight, I bounced upon him, savoring every thrust. The summer breeze rustled the high grass in which we lay and fluttered the huge oak and maple trees above our deeply tanned, naked bodies. I thrust my hips up, pulling my cock nearly all the way out of Vance's asshole. Then I thrust down again as he wriggled his ass.

"I'm getting close, Vance."

"Come in me, Rick," he gasped. "Oh, just let me get off with you. I want another anal orgasm."

I humped him harder as the tingles raced through the head of my cock. "If you don't shoot your cum, I'll suck you after I finish," I promised. The tingles grew until I was thrusting maniacally in his ass. I humped him up and down, filling Vance and emptying him faster than the incubus of his wildest dreams.

"Ah, keep it up, Rick. Fuck my ass until I come."

Alas, I was fated to come too soon, or he too late. The rapture of full orgasm was upon me. Instead of reducing pleasure, the condom tight on my dick enhanced the experience. The muscles at the base of my cock were contracting rhythmically, spurting cum into the condom.

"Give it to me. Give it to me." Vance was virtually shrieking as I pumped my cum. But there was a third voice added to the mix.

"No, boys. No. No." The voice was actually shrieking with priggish disapproval. "You can't do that here. Never. Never."

The afterglow of orgasm ruined, I pulled my cock out of Vance's ass and rolled over.

Rooster Rock is a basalt obelisk, located in an Oregon state park along the Columbia River about twenty-five miles east of Portland. Lewis and Clark camped there in 1805, but they used the original Chinook word *iwash*, meaning Cock Rock, since the monolith resembled not a chicken but an upraised penis. Later the name was changed to Rooster Rock to avoid offending any prudish, namby-pamby, pantywaisted citizens.

During the summer months, I spend every weekend at Rooster Rock's officially designated clothing-optional beach. With its secluded coves and inlets off the Columbia River, its miles of foot trails through the tall grass and among the thick willows and blackberry canes, sandy beaches, and sun-draped dunes, the park is a paradise of men. Yes, some women sun in the nudist area, but the long hike from the parking lot through the wild roses and the willows beyond the prying eyes of the family beaches discourages most. On a summer weekend, the eye lingers over a sea of naked gay men, their bodies growing browner and browner under the yellow rays.

There is an etiquette to nude beaches that can be stated in a single command: don't fuck it up for everybody else. That means no sex, primarily. Nobody violated that rule on the beach, but back in the bushes the breaches occurred. There was a hardcore group who went for sex with wanton disregard for the Edenic purity of other nudists. I had never thought myself one of their number until I met Vance.

He had spread his blanket in a meadow, secluded by wild roses and encroaching willows, and was lolling face down on it. His deeply tanned buttocks lured me. The spicy scent of Oregon grape tantalized my nostrils as I stood over him. I guessed that he was about my own age, perhaps thirty. Young enough to retain the last blush of youth and old enough to have developed some skill. At first I stared, lust rising in my heart, in my thoughts, and in my cock. Inching closer, I let my shadow slide across his profiled face.

Soon we were talking as if we had known each other for years. While we exchanged secrets, his eyes wandered over my body. It seemed that he talked to my cock only—not that I minded. I was hard with desire for his ass.

"Do you want to fuck me, Rick?" he asked suddenly.

A bolt shot through me. Here was an offer to do exactly what I should not do. Anonymous sex on the beach. A violation of nudist etiquette. Inappropriate activity that would further diminish the reputation of Rooster Rock and would reflect upon all naturists.

"Yeah," I said, fingering the head of my engorged cock. It was so stiff that I was on the verge of coming already. "I do."

With a wicked grin, Vance produced a bottle of lubricant. He slicked my dick and slipped an extra-strength condom onto it. I was not about to enter him abruptly; though my cock was swollen painfully, I took my time exploring his body. I kissed the nape of his neck. His back was muscled, so I could follow a pattern with my fingers while I traced his spine with my lips.

His cleft was deep, his buttocks massive. I drove my face down his anal crevice, probing aggressively with my tongue. Vance moaned with enraptured delight.

I could bear the pressure no longer. My balls were tight and painful, my cock so engorged that it threatened to split open if it did not spit. Taking the lubricant, I slid a slick finger into Vance's ass. He moaned again. "Yeah, Rick, do me that way."

I lubricated my finger again and twisted it in Vance's ass. He wiggled his rump with explicit invitation. Two fingers slid in easily; I opened him up and made him slick.

Vance emitted a long howl, sounding like a feral creature in heat. "I'm ready to take it, Rick."

"I know." I barked a short laugh. Climbing atop him, I pressed the head of my cock against his asshole. "It's going in." Vance drew a deep breath as I pushed into him. His ass opened around me, though he fit me tightly.

"What a rectum you have, Vance," I panted. "What a perfect fit. It's like sticking my cock into a toaster. You're hot, tight, and grainy." I thrust, savoring the friction.

"Oh, ah, I'm coming." Vance was wiggling and squeezing my cock as he shot his load onto his blanket.

He had come so quickly that I scarcely managed ten strokes in his ass before his contractions and the odor of his spent cum sent warnings of oncoming orgasm rippling through my cock. I could have stopped then, made it last, but I did no such thing. I went for the pleasure. I thrust harder, humping Vance's tight ass with all my might. My cock was carried up into a whirlwind of tingles that spun up my shaft and whipped my balls. The muscles at the base of my cock contracted inflexibly, a biting burst. I shot so hard that had Vance not insisted on protection, my cum would have traveled like a bullet through his digestive tract, knocking out his front teeth as it shot out of his mouth.

Or such was my fantasy as I shot spurt after spurt into his ass while the sun beat down on my bare back, legs, and ass and the scents of wild rose, big river, and grape opened my senses to the rapture.

Afterward we washed the tools of our sexuality in the river. The eyes of many naked men followed us, knowing eyes that recognized a milked cock and a fresh-fucked ass. Seeking solitude, Vance took my hand and we waded across the shallows to Sand Island, which is also clothing-optional.

Large dunes rise on the river side of the island, but most of it is heavily forested. Hand in hand we climbed the dunes to get a better view of the nude sunbathers who had taken over the island. "Look at the ass on that guy," I remarked, pointing toward a delicious specimen lying face down on his blanket.

"Check out that guy's cock," Vance said simultaneously, indicating a different sun worshiper.

"We're a perfect match," I said.

"You're a top, and I'm a bottom," Vance replied with a giggle. Still laughing, we descended from the dune and strolled along the beach decorated with blankets, ice chests, beach umbrellas, and naked men.

Vance and I spent the summer fucking like minks (gay minks—minks born with rainbow triangles on their heads). One bright day in late August, we were banging away in our secret meadow under the wild rose not far from the swift river, which opened us up to the rude intrusion of the beach patrol.

"Give it to me," Vance kept gushing. "Give it to me."

"No, boys. No. No."

Rolling off Vance's ass, I shot most of my load into the air.

"You can't do that here. Never. Never."

I looked up at him. "Who the fuck are you?"

"I'm Winston. I'm a member of the beach patrol." He lifted his yellow flag in demonstration.

I gave Winston the once-over. He was rather tall, but he had the shortest cock I had ever seen stuck on a human male. His naked skin was deeply tanned, as if he spent every single day patrolling the nude beach. He had narrow shoulders but a pronounced chest. He had nice-looking legs that went all the way up to a set of cute buttocks. I guessed that he was, perhaps, five years younger than Vance and I.

While we appraised his assets and his shortages, Winston delivered a detailed spiel about how Rooster Rock had declined during the last decade of the twentieth century as invasive willows had covered the meadows and dunes, giving shelter to illicit behaviors such as homosexual activity, voyeurism, and alcohol-or-drug-related violence. Naturist families interested in social nudism drifted toward Sauvie Island's family-friendly nude beach, abandoning Rooster Rock to the undesirable elements.

"Meaning us?" I asked. "We're undesirable elements?"

"Your day in the sun has run its course," Winston proclaimed. "Family-oriented social nudism is returning to the Rock. The beach patrol has arrived to flush out the degenerates and perverts who ruin the experience for everyone."

Out of the corner of my eye, I could see Vance's lips twitching. He was trying not to laugh at Winston's diatribe, and about to fail miserably. I shot him a wink and a significant look. Quick on the uptake, Vance caught on immediately. While I jumped to my feet and circled behind Winston, Vance rose to his knees and reached for the underside of Winston's balls.

"Oh, my!" Winston yelped. "You must not."

As Vance rubbed Winston's perineum, Winston dropped the yellow flag he had been displaying so prominently and began to display a different tool.

Winston cried out again, but more softly: "Oh, what are you trying to make me do?" I do not think he expected an answer. His enjoyment was patently obvious. Yes, Winston's tiny cock hardened to its full four inches. He kept whimpering that our actions were impermissible, yet at the same time, through deed rather than word, he permitted all and invited more.

I wasn't entirely successful in suppressing a giggle, but truth to tell, his small penis was downright cute. And his ass was even better up close. He had a nice swell, a good rounded moon shape that made me want to caress it. Vance was still rubbing the underside of Winston's balls, giving the man from the beach patrol an external prostate massage. He was also tweaking Winston's cockhead with two fingers. So I gave in to my lust and explored Winston's ass.

Thus far Winston had stood frozen except for a few shattered protests, huffs, and wheezes, but when I ran my thumb up his anal cleft, he surrendered with a sharp intake of breath that resembled nothing less than a backward howl.

I was a bit loud in my joyous exclamation. "Winston, you're a butt boy."

"Oh, we shouldn't be doing this," Winston managed, pushing his ass back. "Oh mighty Zeus, I'm doing the very thing I've been fighting against."

"Isn't that always the way, Winston?" I kissed the small of his back and let my tongue graduate slowly and inevitably into his butt crack. I stopped only to philosophize: "We always end up doing or becoming the thing we resist the hardest."

"Oh, no, I can't be doing this," Winston yelped. I touched my tongue to his asshole and felt the shudder of total surrender. "Don't do it," Winston wailed. "Don't stop. I want you inside me. I want your cock in my ass. I want you to fuck me."

"Winston, you're just like me," Vance shouted with delight.

As he fiddled with Vance's dick and balls, he intoned mindlessly, "We're here; we're queer; we take it in the rear."

Vance and I got Winston down on our blanket. The perfume of previously spilled cum mingled with the fragrances of the wide river, the pools of standing water, and the trees. Winston breathed deeply of these odors and writhed in utter rapture as we brought him close to orgasm, time after time, without letting him fall into quick bliss.

"Fuck me, guys. I want it."

"Sure, Winston," I promised. "You're gonna get stuffed." I did want his ass. It was cute and utterly desirable. However, I had a scheme that I had been wanting to try, and this seemed the perfect opportunity.

"I'll slip a condom on your cock, Rick," Vance offered.

"No, Vance, how about I put the condom onto your dick. I want you to give it to Winston."

"I'm not a top."

"You can do it, Vance." I pointed toward Vance's cock, which was thick, hard, and ready to go, and then I pointed toward Winston's four-inch erection. "You've got more than two inches on him. This time you're gonna pitch."

"Yeah, pitch it to me, Vance," Winston urged. "I'm not designed to pitch, but you are. You've got six and a half inches of solid meat." Winston fiddled with his little cock and then pointed toward his girlish ass. "I'm built to catch."

Protesting no further, Vance let me prepare his cock for action. He climbed onto Winston and rubbed his cock between Winston's prominent buttocks. "I've only tried this once," Vance confessed, "and it didn't work out." However, he kept humping, and his cock looked as if it had grown even more rigid, were that possible.

"It's gonna work out really well this time," I suggested.

The scene was making me hot. I fingered my cock head while I watched Vance position his cock against Winston's asshole and drive it inside. I'd shot my cum into Vance not thirty minutes before, but I was ready to go again. Why not jerk off while I watched Vance fuck Winston?

I poured lubricant into my palm and slicked my fingers. Gripping my cock shaft, I beat my meat while Vance rode Winston. Turning his head toward me as he squeezed Vance's cock with his anal sphincter, Winston saw that I was jacking off. Can you believe it? The man winked at me. Giving me a few seconds to twist the head of my cock as though I were opening a bottle, he snitched, "Your friend is flogging his dolphin."

"Oh, you pervert, Rick," Vance gurgled.

Laughing, I jerked my dick toward his face. "Want a facial, Vance?"

"Give it to me." My beloved humped harder. Considered all the options. "Oh, next time." Decided where my cum should go. "Give it to Winston now." Found his measure and his depth. "He needs it worse than I do."

"Oh, you're giving it to me, Vance," Winston moaned, oblivious of all else. "You're sticking it to me so good, and I love taking it."

Blissful tingles raptured up my cock. I jacked and screwed my cockhead with my fist as the pleasure mounted. "I'm gonna come on your face, Winston. Here it comes. Taste it."

Pounding my cock toward Winston's panting mouth, I savored the ripples fluttering through my cockhead, along the shaft, and even up my ass. My nipples crinkled as the full force of orgasm struck. My lips twitched and my eyelids fluttered. Then my muscles contracted, and a spurt of cum hit Winston's upper lip. Winston grinned with pleasure as he licked his lips, all the while hunching his ass up to meet Vance's frenzied thrusts.

I came more than I would have believed possible. It was, after all, my second ejaculation, with thirty minutes in between. Hot spurts of cum decorated Winston's lower face and jaw line. After my last shot, I pressed my cock against Winston's lips so he could lick the last drops. Engaged as I was, I did not hear the rustling of the tall grass nor feel the shadow that passed over me. Winston did, but he was still pinned under Vance, who was luxuriating in Winston's ass with the afterglow of orgasm. I heard the voices at the same time Winston turned his face away from my cock.

"No, boys. No. No. You mustn't engage in homosexual acts in the bushes. Never. Never." The two naked women who had caught us were pointing at Vance's ass with their yellow flag. My cum dripping from his chin, Winston favored the women with a sickly look.

"Winston!" one gasped. "Not you! You're supposed to be setting an example."

Vance pulled his cock out of Winston's ass. Winston's anal sphincter gave a popping sound as it emptied. Vance pulled the cum-filled condom off his dick. Obliging, one of the women held out her waste disposal sack so he could drop the condom in with the other effluvia that the patrol had cleaned from the beach.

The consequences of our exposure were hideously ironic. The patrol let Vance and me off with a warning, while they banned Winston for life. Since he had been one of their number, his fall was the greater crime in their eyes. Not that this minor disaster affected our lives much. Vance and I never had sex on the beach again, mainly because we did want to support the naturist cause. Giving the anti-nudism forces another reason to restrict the human spirit was in no one's interest.

Instead, Vance and I switched our activities to a gay bathhouse where no one minded what we did. Frequently, Winston joined us, which kept me terribly busy since Vance still preferred catching to pitching. After all, what is a top supposed to do with two bottoms?

MIX AND MATCH

Dominic Santi

My job is fucking sweet. Ever since I started grad school, I've taken a summer hiatus to work as a lifeguard at the county park. I spend my days perched in my tower, surveying my domain, or swimming in cool, clear river water that's so pure I damn near feel guilty peeing in it. My business attire is a loose white tank top and comfortably baggy trunks that show off the form I've maintained since I led my college water polo team to Nationals. The bright red shorts let my balls breathe, yet hint at the respectable size of my cock. Designer shades are a reimbursable business expense once a season. Sunscreen is provided at no cost. All summer long, hordes of gorgeous young things from the local university come to strut their stuff along my hot sandy beach. And every July, the university's international exchange programs swing into high gear.

It's like having the fucking United Nations banging at my door. I've done and been done by every shade of brown, black, white—hell, there's even been tangerine a couple times when somebody got carried away with faux tan lotion. They swim in my river, sleek toned bodies gliding through the water and playing in the waterfall where Wolf Creek tumbles over a low granite ledge and into the main part of the river. And when they think I can't see them, they drop their trunks in the shade of the trees behind the farthest changing room and suck each other off with an uninhibited enthusiasm that puts every porno I've ever seen to shame.

The scenery here is downright beautiful. Last week I was in love with a Costa Rican volleyball team. They set up nets in the sand for their practice games. For four solid days, I was treated to a display of hard, brown, competitive bodies leaping and diving while I dreamed of being the hot, blond sand spraying up between their legs and into their crotches. Since I was on duty the whole fucking time the team played, my fantasies centered pretty heavily on a particularly buff hitter whose shorts rode so low on his ass that he had to keep pulling them up after each awesome jump. I saw just enough of those firm, brown globes to keep my dick drooling. I had plans to bury my face in his crack and lick ass until he begged me to fuck him—and all his buddies, one after the other.

They all had girlfriends—during the day. I was distracted a few times by unsupervised kiddies who, along with their idiot parents, had to be reminded that those who can't swim should not go out into deep water with a current. But once the team and I got to know each other, three of them came back to hang out with me in the evening. I put up the "closed" sign across the entrance to the parking lot. Despite my execrable Spanish, once we were stripped down and skinny dipping, I got my ideas across pretty well.

The water in the pool at the base of the waterfall was warm enough to be comfortable, even as the shadows deepened. I lined up José, Ernesto, and dream boy hitter, Hermán, so they were holding onto outcroppings on the low rock wall along the outer edges. As they floated on their backs, hands firmly gripping the wall, I moved between José's open legs and crouched into the chest-deep water. I cupped his balls and peeled back his long, smooth, coffee-colored foreskin. As he moaned and arched into my mouth, I bathed the last of the salty tang from his warm, hidden folds. When he was twitching and moaning and his silky sensitive dickhead was so hard it poked free of its cover all on its own, I filled my mouth with cool water and sucked in his cock.

José came so hard he yelled. His buddies thought that was hilarious. Turns out he really thought he was straight and that was the first time he'd ever had a man's mouth on his dick. Whatever. His friends can help him get past his straight-boy illusions later. In the meanwhile, I segued into doing Ernesto and Hermán. They both wanted their cocks sucked and their assholes rimmed and a good, hard fuck up the ass while they came. Rubbers work in the water, so I was glad to oblige, eventually shooting my own high, white arc of spunk while I floated alongside the wall with Hermán's fingers up my ass and Ernesto jacking my dick and even straight-boy José kissing me like he couldn't get enough of my tongue.

The following week, I had a Japanese computer science major on his first trip away from home, a tenured Native American Lit professor, and a couple of USMC officer candidates who were as pearly white as my sorry ass. On Tuesday, within an hour of each other, but on different breaks, I sucked off an Egyptian and fucked an Israeli behind the same shrub by the changing rooms. Later on, as I slathered Caladryl on my knees, I wondered if they'd run into each other at the health clinic when they were getting their poison sumac treated. They were both going to be considerably more affected than I was, though I was still careful to use vague terms as to where on my person I'd been "poisoned" when I put in the emergency maintenance request to get the offending plants removed.

It took a week of no sex to get back to normal, and when I returned to work I had to spend five days of mandatory full-time making nice to a group of middle-aged tourists in town for a married couples' religious retreat. Boring! Although age is not an issue for me, anyone with potential in that group was way too obviously shackled to someone with a pussy.

When their bus finally drove off into the distance, I heaved a sigh of relief and tossed their "Remind us to come back next year!" postcard into the trash. If they wanted to have another dedicated lifeguard assigned to them, I wasn't going to volunteer for the job. They could make reservations on the county's fucking website.

By the time I got back to the beach, I was horny as hell. Clouds were rolling in and the weather report on the tower radio said rain was on the way. To me, unless it's a thunderstorm, rain has never been a reason to stay out of the water. I mean, hell, I'm going into the water to get wet, you know? But the guests usually scatter when the sky starts getting dark.

I climbed back into my chair, surprised to see a single man still wading along the edge of the water. His khaki slacks were rolled up to mid-calf and he carried leather dress shoes and dark socks in one midnight-black hand. His short-sleeved shirt blew back in the breeze and his short, tightly curled hair glistened lightly with sweat. I like looking at a well-dressed man, but the taut body under this man's clothes was what interested me. A hard-on the size of Montana was tenting the front of his pants. And he was smiling at me.

The closer he got, the more his white teeth split the darkness of his gorgeous, strong face. By then, I recognized him. Thomas and I had taken a class together a couple of years before. We'd fucked our brains out one long, blissful night after a party honoring him as teaching assistant of the year for the School of Business. He'd been a distance runner in college and he still ran marathons. We'd had an ongoing friendly disagreement over who had more stamina and talent, swimmers or runners. He'd offered to teach me to run marathons and I'd offered to teach him how to really swim. But right now, the only sport I was interested in with him was fucking. I knew just how good his cock felt sliding up my ass.

"I thought you'd gone back to Kenya!" I laughed, sliding down onto the sand. One quick look around assured me we were definitely the only ones on the beach.

"I did," he smiled, his eyes traveling deliberately down and back up my body as we shook hands. "I'm back for some postdoc work. The department chair suggested I visit the beach to relax." Thomas's rich British accent slid over my skin, his grip firm as he held onto my hand way longer than was necessary. "I didn't expect to find you here. Do you still shave your entire body, swimmer boy?"

"The better to slide against you—if you've a mind to fuck."

Thomas's grin matched mine as he cupped his crotch lecherously, letting me know exactly where his mind was. The sky was darkening quickly now. I could smell the rain coming on. With a final glance around the empty beach, I flicked off the radio and hung the huge "Beach Closed Due to Weather" sign on my chair. Then I grabbed my bright red lifeguard towel and my backpack and led Thomas to the thick copse of trees on the other side of the changing rooms—the side where even someone in the lifeguard stand couldn't see us and where I'd verified that there was no fucking poison sumac.

I was hard just thinking about how good it was going to feel being fucked by him again. I spread my towel at the base of a huge overhanging tree. Thomas tossed his shoes and socks onto the sand. Then he jerked me into his arms and shoved his tongue down my throat.

Fuck, Thomas knew how to kiss. He tasted spicy and sweet, like cardamom and tea. I groaned as the heat of his body seeped into my skin. The muscles in his arms and legs were like steel ropes. Everywhere his skin touched me, it felt like I was being brushed with warm, soft velvet.

"Lose the pants, pretty boy."

Thomas's hands slid up to hold my head. With our tongues wrestling like anacondas, I shucked my trunks off and kicked them to the side. It felt weird standing outside in broad daylight in just my tank top, kissing someone who was fully dressed. But it was also way fucking hot. His hands slid down to cup my ass. I shivered hard.

"Kneel on the towel with your face down and your arse in the air." Thomas's breath was cool on my wet lips. I was so addled from that incredible fucking kiss I couldn't think of anything to say. I just nodded and knelt on the towel with my forehead on the thick, soft terry cloth and my ass pointed up at the sky. Thomas laughed as he knelt down beside me. From the corner of my eye, I saw his neatly ironed pants framed by the bright red of the towel. The outline of his gorgeous erection was right in my line of sight. He pushed my shirt up and out of the way.

"One would think a lifeguard would make time to get an all-over tan." His voice dripped mock disapproval as his hand slid over my hip.

"Fuck you. When I'm naked, I'm too busy socializing to sunbathe." I moaned as his fingers slid into my crack. "Lube's in my backpack."

"Still well-prepared," he chuckled. The backpack zipper

whizzed open. "Your arse is an interesting shade of pale, consid-ering how tan your legs are—and your back."

"I don't always wear my shirt." This time his fingers were slippery when they slid into my crack. I groaned loud and long. Thomas laughed again.

"I'd wager you don't wear your pants that often, either. This bottle is half-empty." His finger slid in, hard and demanding, and it stayed there while he stroked his thumb over my perineum. "Do you remember when we fucked before?"

"Oh, yeah!" I wiggled my ass at him, squeezing his finger as my dick twitched at the stimulation. I'd taken a lot of dicks in my life, but his was one of the few that had ever really filled me.

"Then you'll remember I like to play before I fuck, so your hole is relaxed enough to take me without turning into a bloody tourniquet."

"I remember." My train of thought flew out the window as Thomas unzipped his pants. He wasn't wearing underwear. As soon as his fly was open, his long, thick cock fell out, waving purplish black and heavy, the foreskin already stretching back over the glistening head.

I licked my lips. "I want to suck your dick."

Thomas's laugh was low and musical. "I believe that's my cue to remove my clothing."

I squirmed in frustration as his fingers pulled free. The sight of Thomas sitting on the towel beside me, baring his ropes of arm and leg muscle and the hard wall of his chest and abs had my dick throbbing harder than ever. His cock jutted up, stiff and mouth-wateringly close. He folded his shirt and pants into a pile, taking a condom from his pocket and setting it on the towel. Then he lay down beside me, with his feet at my head. He pulled my leg over him and yanked me down so my cock bobbed against his chest. His beautiful dark cock arched up towards me, the smell of his musk filling my nostrils as I licked my lips. Then he cupped a buttcheek in each hand and pulled. As my asshole stretched, he put his thumbs on either side of my still-slippery ass lips and started to rub.

"Suck my cock."

I did not have to be told twice. I opened my mouth and dragged my tongue down the length of his shaft. His skin was soft and warm and salty over the rigid flesh beneath. Thomas slowly stretched me open, drowning my ass in lube as he worked his fingers into me and pulled in deep, relentless circles. When his fingers again slid into me, I opened my mouth as wide as I could, took a deep breath, and swallowed his cock.

His hiss of pleasure was all the incentive I needed to keep my throat around his cock until I was ready to pass out from lack of air. I'd enjoyed Thomas's company before, in class and after the party. I was actually interested in what he'd been doing since I'd seen him last. But there was no way in hell I was going to let go of that delicious dick for anything as mundane as talking. We could do that later. As I once more choked in a breath, I wrapped my hands around the dark, wrinkled sack that held his low hanging balls and tugged on the tight, black curls. He arched up into my throat, his fingers sliding into me again; I couldn't even guess how many he had stuffed up my ass.

"Your arsehole is definitely ready to be fucked."

Understatements R' Us. He slapped my ass. I pulled up and turned around, squatting over him with my feet planted firmly on the towel, my hands braced for balance. Thomas pulled on the condom and slathered it with lube. Using both hands, he held his cock steady as I slowly lowered myself onto him.

He was slick and I was ready, but when his dickhead popped through, it still felt like I was being split in two. I hissed and stiffened, my eyes watering. But I was so horny, I didn't stop. I wanted his fucking dick up my ass, and I wanted it now. Thomas didn't say anything, just stared at me with his huge, brown, velvety eyes and that smile creasing his lips. He held his cock rock-still as it slowly speared up into me. My dick had softened, but the hungry look he was giving me combined with the glorious feeling of his cock sliding through my hole had me getting hard all over again. I groaned as my asscheeks brushed against his pubic hair.

"My ass is so full," I whispered, trying to squeeze his cock with my ass. I was stretched too wide to give him much more than a little hug. Precum oozed up from my joyspot.

"I'm in the mood for a long, slow fuck." His low laugh felt like it was vibrating right through me. "Feel free to come whenever you want. I doubt it will make any difference in the tightness of your arsehole anymore." Putting his hands on my waist, he helped me slowly raise up and lower myself back down.

My hole was so stretched he could have driven a truck through it, and I was so turned on I figured I was going to last about twenty seconds. But the pace Thomas set was slow and steady and such excruciating bliss that rather than sending my dick into a cum frenzy, my body felt like it was gradually being teased into exploding from the inside out. My ass and balls and chest and shoulders, hell, even my fucking ears trembled as much as my legs. I raised and lowered myself again and again, staring down between my burning thighs at my sweat pouring down onto his glistening black abs. His thighs flexed beneath me, tensing with each thrust. My cock bobbed over him, red and drooling precum.

"Show me your infamous swimmer's stamina." Sweat ran down Thomas's face and torso, but that fucker was still laughing as he wrapped his long, dark fingers around my hairless white balls. I lifted my chin, ready to show him I could last as long as any fucking runner could, no matter how turned on I was. Then that fucker cheated. He wrapped his other hand around my dick. His fingers were slippery with lube and he started jacking me off.

I barely recognized the sound coming from my throat as mine. Just like that, he'd won, and I did not fucking care. I lifted up, his cock once more burning through my hole as his hand stroked relentlessly over my shaft. My balls were climbing my dick.

"Let it happen," he said softly. I sank down, his cock once more filling my ass. He twisted his hand over my dick. Fuck, fuck, FUCK! Shaking and shouting, I ground against him, putting my full weight on him as creamy ropes of jism jetted out onto his chest. I literally saw fucking stars. Thomas grabbed my waist, his arm muscles bulging as he lifted me just enough to rabbit punch his cock up into me. Each bludgeoning thrust forced more cum out of me, until my whole body felt like one howling, shuddering orgasm. He shouted as he came, his huge cock stretching my poor battered hole even farther.

My legs were shaking too hard to support my weight anymore. I eased forward, until Thomas's cock pulled free with a soft plop. Then I collapsed onto him, so fucking wasted I could hardly breathe. My heart pounded against his, my cum drying between us as he stroked my back. No coach on land or water had ever put me through a more exhausting workout.

The rain had started. Occasional drops fell through the leaves and onto our sweaty skin. When I'd finally caught my breath, I rolled over next to Thomas, stretching like a well-petted cat. Then I tipped my head back to catch the drops falling through the leaves. I glanced at him from the corner of my eye.

"So does this mean you're ready to learn to really swim now?

You're pretty lucky, you know. I'm a lifeguard and a certified swimming instructor. Hell, I'm a certified water polo coach."

As usual, Thomas was smiling. "I presume that means you're qualified to show me how to handle balls underwater."

I turned and gave him a big, slurping kiss. "You bet your ass. Want to get wet?"

"Later," he growled, grabbing me and sliding his fingers back into my well-used hole. "For the moment, we're practicing stamina."

I kissed him back. With a little bit of rest, I was going to be up for him taking me wherever he wanted to go. Rain or shine, the "Beach Closed" sign was staying up for the rest of the day.

THE ULTIMATE BREAKUP CURE

Raven de Hart

L ying bitch." I tossed a rock at the ocean, sending up a shower of gems in the sunset.

Penny pressed a bottle of Patrón into my hand. "You need a whole lot more of this."

"I don't want any." I really did, and swilled down so much tequila I coughed it all down my front. "I did everything for him. His stupid fucking car? I had my dad fix it up for him when we graduated college. Do you know what he got me? A card! That job he has? I recommended him to my cousin in the first place." I kicked through the sand, showering the bonfire in particles. "Then that bastard sold the store and the new owner won't fire him."

I grabbed for the liquor again, but Penny pushed my hand away. "Hell no." She wrapped her arm around me. "Luke, you're a good guy and Kenny's a total ass."

"You're my hag. You have to say that." I still nuzzled closer to her. "But thanks."

She squeezed me tighter, then got up and tossed a new log on the fire. "What you need is to get right back up on the whore."

"Horse."

She shook her head. "No, whore. Find some guy and have him fuck your brains out, drink a glass of orange juice, and do it all over again."

I couldn't help but laugh, and I really tried not to. "Hard sweaty sex isn't the answer to all of life's problems, Pen."

"No, but it's *normally* a good idea." She sat down and sipped at the tequila. Then she opened her mouth, tugged on my sleeve, and pointed. I was a bit delirious, so it took me a minute to follow her finger to the spectacle. She finally got out her word. "Damn."

I had to agree. You know those fan-service scenes with the guy walking down the beach at sunset? Well, that's what it was. He had store-bought, bleach-blond hair, long legs, and that body. "Damn."

Penny tugged even harder at my sleeve. "Luke, he's coming this way."

I laughed. "Fat chance. He's probably just headed back to his car or something." He stepped closer. "Or he's lost and looking for directions."

"Have a little faith, Luke. He's coming *right to us*."

Fuck. Fuck fuck fuck. He was. He stopped just in front of the fire. "You guys mind if I chill here for a sec?"

"No." Penny got off the log. "It's warmer over here, if you're cold."

"Thanks."

I tried to follow her, but she pushed me down. The stranger sat closer than I expected—he *was* kind of cold. "Sorry for intruding." He extended a hand to me, a tattooed chain winding over his skin. "Sean."

"Luke." I stayed in the handshake longer than I should have, only letting go when he cleared his throat. I shook myself back to functionality. "Right, that's Penny."

"You mean the girl? She just went to the bathroom."

Bitch. "Oh, well, her name's still Penny."

He leaned in close, so I could feel his breath on my face. "Hey, man, what's wrong?"

"What do you mean?"

He ran a finger just under my eye. "You've been crying."

I shook my head. "It's nothing." I looked around for some way to change the subject and found the tequila. After taking a hearty helping, I offered it to Sean. "It'll warm you up."

"Yeah, thanks, man." He sipped it and started hacking and coughing. "Damn, that must be good tequila." He handed it back, face red. "Never could stomach that stuff too well."

"Yeah, it's not my favorite either, but it was an emergency drinking situation." Damn it. I'd actually managed to change the subject, and then I just went and threw away the effort. "So what are you doing out here?"

He sighed. "I like it out here this time of the evening, with the sun on the water and all that. It's pretty."

"So are you."

Shit. One too many drinks tonight. I stammered, but Sean rolled with it. "Well you ain't exactly hideous yourself." He hugged me. Apparently, in his mind, that was okay. Of course, I didn't argue, so what does that say? Mind you, I *was* trying to fight back some serious boner action, so I at least had some excuse. He let go. "When did you get dumped?"

A chill ran across my face. "How the hell did you know?"

"I'm psychic." He laughed, digging into the pocket of his jean shorts. "No, I found this picture torn up down on the other end of the beach."

It was a shot of me and Ken from Christmas, wearing nothing but Santa caps. I grabbed it and tossed it in the fire. "This morning."

"Tough break."

"We were together since high school." I took another big drink of Patrón. "Come to find out he's been nailing my sister on his lunch break for the past two years."

"Ouch."

"You don't have to tell me."

We sat there for a while until Penny came back. "Who died?" she asked, looking at how glum Sean and I were.

I looked up at her. "My relationship."

"Yeah, but what else?"

Sean stretched, yawning. "Well, thanks for the fire. I should leave you two be."

He started back along the beach and a word leaped from my throat. "Wait!" He turned and Penny laughed. I slapped her across the shoulder. "You can stick around, if you don't have anything better to do." My face got even hotter as I spoke. "I mean, just a suggestion."

"Not a suggestion." Penny bull-rushed into control, yanking Sean back towards the logs. She dropped him in my lap. I gave her the best "you're not helping" look I had, but she carried on, digging her car keys out of her pocket. "I can walk from here to my brother's. You two take my car somewhere and talk, and I'll pick up it up from Luke in the morning."

I shook my head as Sean shimmied off me and onto the log. *Dear God, don't let him have noticed the hard-on.* "I don't think that's the best idea, Pen. I've had a long, bad day."

"Well, misery loves company, right?" Sean gave me a lopsided grin. "But I'm not comfortable taking your car, Penny." He stretched, sun-darkened skin tightening across his ribs. "It's a nice night. We can just stay here and talk." He gestured to me with the near-empty bottle of Patrón. "Unless you don't want to."

I shrugged, trying to marry two conflicting choices. I didn't *want* another relationship, especially with a guy I didn't know, but couldn't convince my dick—and he was winning out. "I have tomorrow off, so I guess I can stick around for a bit."

"Great." Penny fished out her cell phone. I knew what she was doing, but didn't have time to stop her. "Shit. Turns out my brother isn't home at all—he's out at a bar and needs me to pick him up." She winked at me. "I should be back in an hour or two."

I sighed and turned back to Sean. "I guess we have some time, then."

He chuckled. "She's not very subtle, is she?"

"She likes to think she is."

He scuffed his sandals in the sand. "Would it really be that bad if we had sex?"

"Wait, what?"

"I mean, sorry, I shouldn't have said that." He busied himself, throwing another couple of logs on the fire. The sparks that burst out of the flames clouded him, making him look like a dream.

A very good, very *bad* dream.

He sat next to me in total silence, staring into the fire, across the ocean, at the first speckling of stars—just not at me. Finally, I had to laugh. "It's really okay."

Sean said, "I've just always been cool with sex, and sometimes I forget not everyone is."

I chugged the last eighth-inch of tequila and scooted closer. He smelled like wet sand and sweat. I kissed his cheek, running my tongue along the upper line of his jaw. What? It seemed like the thing to do at the time, and he tasted really good—like seawater. What the hell? It's not like I *didn't* need to get laid.

Sean wrapped his arm over my shoulder, whispering, "Change of heart?"

"I figure." I undid my belt buckle. "There's no harm." Unzipped my fly. "In having a little fun."

He laughed. "How much tequila did you have?"

I was pants-free and working on my shirt at that point. "Enough."

Without warning, with my hands still caught up in trying to get out of my shirt—it's much harder when you're drunk—Sean leaned in and kissed me, sliding his tongue through my lips, running it on the inside of my cheeks. I tasted something sweet. We stayed like that until my arms got tired, then I pulled away. He grinned. "I'm getting a buzz just kissing you."

I finally got off the accursed T-shirt and, panting, looked him over again, just to make sure I *really* wanted to sleep with him. Right, I'm not kidding anyone—I just wanted to look at him some more. He reached down to his crotch and adjusted the bulge, but it didn't do much—the jean shorts were too small and I could see it no matter what he did. I slid closer, wrapping my leg around his, and reached down. "Let me." I wriggled my hand into the warmth between the denim and his coarse bush, making contact with his unit—I could just touch my thumb and middle finger around the shaft. "Damn, Sean. Do you play baseball with it?"

He laughed. "It's a blessing of sorts."

I ran my fingers along the whole length, feeling his veins, drawing tiny circles with my thumb. I kept going further, leaning my body closer to his. My head on his chest, feeling his sharp breaths, then down against his abs, nose against his happy trail. I slipped a finger between his head and foreskin, rubbing all the way around it while fighting the urge to jack off. He moaned a little and I felt it—he was wet. I slowly pulled back out, moving my head down until I reached the zipper on his shorts. I tried to coordinate my tongue to lift it, but the alcohol prevented that. With one move, I pulled down his zipper and pantsed him. Released, his dick wriggled out of the fly of his briefs, precum glistening in the firelight.

I moved my head down, but his hands wrapped over my shoulders, pushing me flat against the log. "That's enough about me." He climbed on top of me, the head of his cock resting against my thigh, precum chilling every time the wind picked up. He breathed right against my mouth, every word traveling through my ears and straight downstairs. "Let's see what you've been hiding." His mouth actually worked—he grabbed the waistband of my underwear in his teeth, pulling them off. The bark of the log scratched my ass and I moved down to the sand while he tossed my now-pointless under-garments aside. I watched his ass roll from side to side, the movement of every muscle visible through the tight fabric. Once he got turned around, he pounced, fingers trailing lust across my chest, pinching my nipples while his tongue danced down, skating warm over my body. He stopped at my waist and, with one heave, put my knees on his shoulders. His hands traced the shape of my ass, one finger straying to the hole, just rubbing around it but never going in. I almost thrust up, aching for something, but he beat me to the punch, shoving his face into my ass. I could see his eyes dance above me as his tongue massaged the entrance open, teasing groans and grunts out of my throat.

When he found his way inside, I just said, "Fuck." The hot snake of muscle pressed and wiggled, opening me further. From what I'd seen so far, I'd need to be open.

He moved away, replacing his tongue with a pair of fingers.

They dug deeper, toying with *the spot*. He dragged them out, pressing against my hole with every knuckle that left. I moaned, shaking with want as the emptiness came over me. He leaned close again, whispering, "Ready?"

I could only nod. He got back in position, lifting my ankles onto his shoulders. The head of his cock rested against my hole for a second, and then he pressed in. My toes and fingers curled, neck tightening. Cold, nervous sweat beaded up on my skin as he made slow, steady progress, the thick shaft filling me. He reached down, rubbing my nipples until they hardened.

I felt bush against my ass and sighed, the ecstasy of fullness radiating from his cock. He smiled, letting me adjust to the size. As I did, warmth flooded my body, electricity that skittered across every pore. I made eye contact and nodded.

As Sean wormed out of me, I nestled deeper into the sand, burying my fingers in the beach. Sean moved in faster, balls slapping against my tailbone. He grunted with every hit, biting his bottom lip to hold back the words. Every once in a while a "fuck" or "hell yeah" would slip out as he went faster still.

When I reached the very edge of my self-control, he pulled out and flipped me on my stomach, digging his fingers into my ass, thumbs resting on the divots on the side. He went back in, each thrust digging me further into the sand. I slipped my hands over my cock and let the force of him fucking me do the work, jacking me off. I still doubted I would last longer than him, but I tried my damnedest to hold back, not wanting it to end. His hand wound into my hair, making it that much harder to keep from coming.

He pulled out and flipped me again, jacking us off together. It just took a few strokes and I shot all over his hand, bucking up and down, sand digging into my ass crack.

He leaned over me and came, losing it all over my chest and

belly. It lasted at least two minutes, both of us shooting off. I gave him one answer. "Damn."

He flopped down next to me, hand lying across my junk. "Ditto."

We lay there naked for a good twenty minutes, talking. I found out he worked as a barista at a local cafe, had a bachelor's in business English, and used to be a hooker. "It's how I paid for college."

Penny came back just when we'd decided to get dressed— we weren't dressed yet, but we'd made the decision. She leaned over me and I screamed. "What the hell?" I shoved my hands between my legs. "Show a little dignity here!"

"I'm not the one lying naked on the beach."

"Bitch." I looked for my underwear, but remembered that Sean had tossed them away. I looked around, but saw nothing. Whatever. I pulled my jeans on, threw on my shirt, and sat up.

Sean already had his shorts on—and a huge grin. "So did your brother get home all right?"

"What?" It took her a bit to remember her lie. "Right, yeah, totally."

"Good." He winked at me. "I guess I might see you around town, right?"

"Maybe. I mean, I do drink coffee."

Back in Penny's car, the interrogation started. "How was it? It was magic, right? Like, totally not human, right?"

I adjusted my dick. "It was good."

"You hit that and you say it was *good*?" She glared for a moment, and then her face brightened. "Oh, I see, it was *good*. Got it."

I still don't know what the fuck she thought I meant.

* * *

I went to Herb's Cafe the next day and waited to see him. Around noon—by that time, five cups of coffee were flooding through my system—he showed up. I got really nervous—he probably wouldn't want to talk to me at work. Hell, maybe he didn't *really* want to talk to me at all.

"Luke." He came straight to me, smiling. I thought I would puke, I was so nervous. "I didn't expect to see you so soon."

"I can go."

"No, it's fine." He sat down at the table. "I called in sick today. Still a little bit sore." He chuckled at his own joke. "How's your headache?" I gestured to the five empty coffee cups. "So, better?"

"Yeah. You want some coffee?"

"No. I actually don't drink coffee." I guess I looked pretty crestfallen, because he stammered out. "But I'll take some tea." He grabbed my hand and led me up to the counter. "Jill."

"Oh, hey, Sean. Let me guess, green tea and honey?"

"And it only took you three months to get it right."

She noticed me for the first time, apparently—never mind that she'd just served me coffee for the past four hours. "Is this the guy?"

Sean shrugged. "Not the time or place, Jill."

"I was just curious. I mean, you talked about him for two hours last night."

I could have been pissed. Maybe I should have been pissed, but I wasn't—hell, at least it meant I was a good lay. I just slung an arm around his shoulder. "Yeah, I'm the guy."

She laughed. "I like him."

With his tea in hand, Sean walked back to the table with me. "So, you're already over your breakup?"

"God no." I sipped at the coffee I'd been nursing for the last hour. "But last night sure helped."

He stared at his tea. "So do you want some more help? Say, tonight?"

I chuckled. "My place or yours?"

WELCOME TO PARADISE

Cecilia Ryan

There was a time when Gene would have said the most beautiful sound on the beach was the crashing of the waves against the shore. That was before he met Dylan, before he was lying next to him after the mad offer of a midnight surf, which had turned into a midnight swim when they realized the water was far too still for it. The soft laughter of the other man, he decided, was the most beautiful sound in the world at the moment.

It was probably better if he didn't say that out loud, though. He didn't think Dylan would react well to being kissed out of the blue—Gene knew he was all for the concept of free love and had no problem with being touched by other men, but for it to be one man, for there to be more than sex involved in it, that would be too much for him. The closest they were ever going to get was with a girl between them, and as much fun as that had been, Gene hadn't been looking at the girl. He couldn't really remember her name, but then she might never have told them.

Gene lay still and turned his head to the side to look at Dylan while he continued to laugh and catch his breath. Even in the moonlight, he could still bring to his mind the sun-kissed hair and sparkling green eyes of his companion. He wished he'd seen him laugh like this in the daytime. This was honest, happy laughter, not the boisterous racket he made for the sake of fitting in. There was nothing insincere in it, and Gene was glad of that. Glad that Dylan trusted him enough to be honest around him.

He watched as the other man turned his head towards him, licking the salt from his lips. Smiling at him. God, he was gorgeous. Gene went to speak, and then the heavens opened instead and buckets of water were suddenly falling on them both. Dylan laughed again and sat up, standing to help Gene so they could take shelter from the rain. Gene took his hand and followed blindly, fighting to keep up with the more lithe man ahead of him, his feet sinking into the sand that had already become waterlogged.

A palm tree provided temporary respite, enough to get a look at the beach and the area around them. Dylan was still laughing brightly, and Gene found himself smiling. Gene chose the beach, the surf, and the lifestyle for the lack of pressure involved; to get away from it all. Dylan chose it out of a genuine love and respect for the elements. Of course he enjoyed the rain as much as the sunshine. It was easy to be happy when Dylan was happy.

"Car?" Gene heard himself suggesting. He didn't especially want this to end, to take Dylan back home and call it a night himself, but it was pouring with rain and there seemed to be little choice. Dylan nodded, and took his hand again to race the rest of the way up the beach and fumble their way into the unlocked station wagon. The rain was so thick that neither of them had realized they were getting into the back seat of the Holden until they'd sat down, both of them laughing hysterically at the mistake and panting to catch their breaths.

Gene found a towel being shoved at him, and dried his hair with it roughly before putting it under himself in an attempt to stop his wet back and shorts from sticking to the seat. It was a wonder that cars like this had leather seats at all. He suspected that they weren't actually leather, but they were just as sticky. By the time he looked back, Dylan was leaning his head against the window and looking at him quietly. Gene smiled, shy without intending to be, and grasped for something to say. "I suppose we're not going anywhere for a while?"

Dylan seemed to come back to life at that. "No, not unless we want to go off the side of a cliff or something." He smiled wryly. "The company could be much worse."

"That it could." Gene nodded honestly. "I'm glad you came out here. Nice to have a fellow countryman to enjoy the rain with."

"No rain like this in England," Dylan replied. "Well, not over the summer, anyway."

"No, I suppose not. More like a constant, miserable drizzle." Gene's lips twitched a little, half amused and half homesick.

Dylan hummed and nodded and then fell silent for a few moments, licking his lips slowly again. After a while, he spoke up hesitantly, "I think I might take these off." He pulled at his soaked shorts. "Dry off and dress. If that's all right?"

"Please, be my guest. I'll let you go first." Gene turned and leaned against the glass, staring out at the storm. He could hear the sounds of Dylan peeling his soaking board shorts off, drying himself, grabbing his clothes and pulling them on. A soft "done" prompted him to look back over, to see that he'd only gotten as far as a pair of boxer shorts and a t-shirt, both equally worn. He didn't look too closely at Dylan's lean thighs or what was between them, instead grabbing his own clothes and going through the same process himself, deciding to follow suit in not bothering with jeans, only pulling on his own wear-softened T-shirt before sitting back down.

When he looked back, he saw Dylan grinning at him. "You have a tan line," he sing-songed. Gene felt himself blush at the statement, more than aware it was true, and realized that Dylan hadn't bothered to look away.

"I suppose you don't?" He balled up the towel he'd been sitting on and stuffed it under the seat in front of him, trying not to think about Dylan's tan line or lack thereof.

"I'm insulted. Do you mean you didn't get a good look at me while we were with Sarah?" Dylan was still grinning, but there was something else in it as well.

Sarah. So she had given her name. Hopefully, he'd remember it if they ran into her again. "That was over a month ago. We didn't know each other then."

Gene hadn't studied the other man at the time, not really. Not that there was much of him he hadn't seen since, but he knew better than to linger. He couldn't look at him as closely as he wanted to, not if he wanted to be his friend.

Or could he? Dylan had looked at him without such a concern, after all. Gene reached out before he realized what he was doing and tugged the waistband of Dylan's underwear down just far enough to check for a tan line. There wasn't one, of course. Dylan was the sort of man who would go down to a quiet cove and lie naked in the sun to get the appealing dark golden color of his skin even. He took his hand away, looking as though there was nothing wrong with what he'd just done. Dylan didn't seem to mind, just watched him calmly as he retreated. "I see."

Dylan grinned at him, clearly pleased with himself. "You should come with me sometime. Get some color in your cheeks."

"Oh, you are hilarious. How did I ever live without your wit, I wonder?" Gene teased, happy to deflect the moment that had become thick and heavy into humor instead, and not think further on the skin of Dylan's hip, smooth and soft as it had been.

"Boringly, I imagine." Dylan sighed at length, closing his eyes. It was a comfortable, soft sound that Gene found left his stomach fluttering. He seemed content, happy to be in his company, even when they were just sitting quietly. They'd never done this before; it had always been go, go, go, or there'd been a huge group sitting in the odd mutual silence that always felt to Gene as though they were communing with the sea, in the strange way the locals had of doing here. He thought perhaps that this was Dylan's influence, since for himself he wouldn't mind if the waves stopped coming tomorrow and the beach was swallowed up—except that he knew it would mean Dylan moving on, and Gene would have no excuse to follow him.

It was a funny thing, love. Prone to catching people at the worst possible moments. He knew that he couldn't afford to fall for anyone, drifters that they both were. Dylan wouldn't stay here over the winter, either. He'd move on to somewhere that was still warm, find a place for his board and another friend to share moments like this with. Gene would become, he knew, another memory—a fond one, cherished even, but a memory nonetheless. Thinking that always made him feel his stomach drop. He was honestly afraid of Dylan moving on before he'd at least taken the chance to see if they could make it together.

"I suppose I must have been," he replied quietly, staring down at his knees so as to avoid looking at Dylan again for the time being. By what seemed like mutual agreement, a silence fell between them while they waited for the rain to ease, which didn't look at all like it was going to happen soon.

By the clock on the dashboard, half an hour passed before Dylan spoke up. "I don't think it's going away any time soon," he said wisely, and Gene was inclined to trust his instincts in this, attuned to nature as he always seemed to be.

"We might as well bunk down for the night, then," Gene tried to keep the enthusiasm out of his voice at the prospect of sharing the close quarters.

"Move out of the way so I can fold these seats down," he instructed. Dylan obeyed without argument, his mouth falling open as the seats were folded down to reveal what was very nearly a full-length bed in the back of the car—Gene had found a foam mattress that fit exactly and folded up easily with the back seat and had grown accustomed to sleeping on it, often having nowhere better to go.

"So *this* is where you sleep." Dylan grinned as though he'd discovered the greatest secret in the universe. "I'd been trying to figure out where you were going off to, but no one seemed to know. S'pose you tend not to invite them back, eh?" He clambered onto the mattress, looking honestly thrilled. Gene understood the feeling—there was something wonderfully comforting and exciting about having what was the equivalent of a childhood fort in the back of your car. He reached into the front to open the window a crack, thankful of the weather shield over the driver's-side window.

Trying not to give too much weight to climbing into the same bed as Dylan, Gene ignored the not-entirely-unpleasant way his stomach clenched as he did so. After a little maneuvering to get comfortable, they came to rest beside each other, heads propped up on hands so they could continue to talk.

"In answer to your earlier question, no. I don't ever share this bed." Gene wasn't sure if that was because it was a private space, or simply because no one would really want him to. He was pleased enough if Dylan drew his own conclusions, though; if he did indeed have a private space, he'd invite Dylan into it, and be happy for him to know that he was doing so.

"Then I'm honored," Dylan replied, and then lowered his eyes almost coyly. "Hasn't been a bad time, all told, has it?" He was biting his lip just softly, and Gene wondered if he realized how gorgeous he was, or if he could truly be ignorant of his own charms.

"Not bad at all. I'm glad you persuaded me to do it." Gene smiled honestly at him and found his smile returned with full force.

"I'm glad I did as well." Dylan reached out, then dropped his hand halfway between them. "We have a lot of fun together, don't we? I mean, I s'pose it's because we're not like the rest of them. I can't understand them half the time, and it's not their accents that're throwing me off, neither."

Gene smiled, fighting to keep a giggle down at Dylan's petulant tone. "Well, if you will come to a place called Surfer's Paradise, you can hardly be surprised when you run into surfers, can you? Especially if you turn up with a board of your own and spend most of your life on the beach, making friends with the other people on said beach. You could hardly expect to run into much else."

Dylan shrugged. "Ran into you, didn't I?"

"That you did. I'm really not like them, am I? Still stick out like a sore thumb, I suspect." Gene found himself smiling shyly once more.

"Not in a bad way. They all love you. Think of you as the clever one. Which is what happens when you start quoting things they've only ever heard of on the telly. Not that I'm about to start asking about your past or anything, but even without the posh accent, you give yourself away a bit."

"Thank you," Gene replied quietly. "For not asking, I mean. I could use a friend I can get close to without having to worry about that."

There was a silence after Dylan nodded, and both men listened to the rain and the rolling thunder coming in from the ocean ahead of them, lightning streaking across the sky in the distance. Gene had heard it was better in the winter. Not quite as warm, but the sun was out more often, and the rain wasn't so heavy, if it rained at all. Funny that the wet season should be in the summer, though. Despite the open window, the car was still getting warm inside, the humidity out there and the heat of two bodies, even at rest as they were, making the air heavy and drowsy. Gene thought to close his eyes, but at some point he'd ended up staring into Dylan's. He wondered if that might have been why the air felt so thick now. He blinked and looked away, turning his head to look out of the rear window at the pelting rain.

Something touched Gene's hair, and it took him a moment to realize that it was Dylan's hand. He didn't dare move his head to look at the other man for fear of startling him out of it, but instead turned all of his other senses toward him, shutting out the sounds and smells of the rain, the heat and weight of the air, and feeling nothing but the gentle pressure of hesitant fingers curling through his salt-stiffened hair, the smell of the sea still clinging to Dylan—as it always did, he supposed—the heat of his breath closer now than it had been. When he concentrated, he could feel that the blond had moved closer to him, almost close enough to touch, but not quite.

"Look at me, Gene." The dark rumble of Dylan's voice rolled over him like the thunder he could barely hear over the pounding in his ears. "Let me see that you want this as much as I do," he whispered, and Gene would have been powerless to stop himself even if he'd been inclined to disobey the command. He turned his head, and Dylan's fingers slid through his hair to cradle it from behind, not truly holding him in place, but supporting.

The first kiss they shared tasted of salt and ozone. The air became too thick to breathe properly after far too short a time, so they retreated to brief kisses, only a handful of seconds long at best, but with each kiss, Gene found he could taste more and more of Dylan. Of the soft, dewy grass he knew back home, and the smoke and fire of the steel works of Dylan's hometown, but also of a sweetness that took him by surprise. Something that reminded him of this place, of the smell of the rainforests after a storm like the one outside, and of sunscreen and aloe gel and everything else that this strange, foreign land had come to mean to him.

Too soon, there wasn't enough air left even for brief kisses, and they both panted harshly, still not touching in more than a few places in deference to the stifling heat. Gene had settled his hand on the soft cotton of the pants that covered Dylan's hip, and there was still a hand in his hair, teasing some of the stiffness out of it.

"God, I want you," Gene panted as he tried to catch his breath, lungs burning with the humid air enfolding them both. "I want you like I've never wanted anything before."

"Why do you think I invited you out tonight?" Dylan asked softly, still stroking Gene's hair. "The day we met, when Sarah dragged you along with me—that was only my second day out here. When I heard you speak, I rolled my eyes. Come all the bloody way out here only to meet some bastard I could have found a few dozen miles away? But what I couldn't get over, while the three of us were at it, was how kind you were.

"Not just a gentleman to her, but you treated me like you wanted me to be there, even though we didn't have a lot of contact. I wished, after, that I'd kissed you. Shown you that I was glad *you* were there, as well as her. You've no idea how happy I was when I realized that you were here on the same sort of holiday I was. That we'd run into each other without me having to come up with excuses."

Gene laughed softly. "Do you know, I thought almost exactly the same thing? I regretted not giving you more attention at the time, but then I thought you might not welcome it, and didn't wish to alienate someone who reminded me of home straight off."

"Homesick?" There was palpable sympathy in Dylan's voice.

"Not really. I don't miss it so much as I feel its loss. Tomorrow, I'll have been gone for two months. In a way it feels like an eternity, but in other ways it's like the blink of an eye. I know I'm not where I'm from at the moment, but I'm also not sure this isn't where I belong." Gene didn't bother to be surprised that he could say these things out loud to Dylan. It was as natural as breathing, more so, even, considering that drawing breath was still difficult, even with the rain finally beginning to clear the air.

Dylan hummed softly. "I know what you mean. But then I don't want to go back, and if I thought there was a way to avoid it, I'd be on it," he admitted, and then smiled. "I could live in the back of this car with you, you know. I'd be happy here."

"I snore," Gene pointed out reasonably.

"So do I. I imagine you make a polite little snort here and there and call it snoring, but I'm told I could wake the dead at fifty paces. Lucky I've learned to wear anyone I'm sharing a bed with out well enough that it doesn't wake them, eh?" He grinned impishly, eyes glittering even in the nearly complete dark that had fallen over them since the automatic light had finally turned itself off.

"Lucky indeed."

Gene honestly didn't mean to react so eagerly to that. Sex wasn't the only thing on his mind when it came to Dylan—he wanted, as his father might have put it, hearts and flowers—though perhaps seashells and board wax would be more appropriate. But if he was being entirely honest with himself, he wanted sex as well. A great deal of it, in fact.

Still grinning, Dylan moved in to kiss him again. It was a gentle kiss, slow and easy enough to breathe through, especially now that the temperature outside was finally dropping. Gene felt the hand in his hair move down, along the back of his neck, over his shoulder, and down the side of his body to his hip. Dylan pushed gently, and Gene gave without protest, rolling onto his back even as the gorgeous blond was moving to straddle him. Narrow hips rocked into his own, and though neither man was fully hard, by the feel of things, Gene could see no need to do anything more than move the hand that had been stroking Dylan's hip earlier up and under his T-shirt to feel along the definite column of his spine, to enjoy the way his strong shoulder muscles shifted under sun-sensitized skin.

"Want you." Dylan kissed over his chin, then along his jaw to his ear, still rocking gently. The entire car was moving with them, and Gene was reminded of what it was like to lie on your back in the ocean, letting the waves take you nowhere in particular. That was what it felt like at the moment, like they weren't going anywhere in particular. He could feel Dylan hard against him, now—a comfortable heat through two thin layers of stretch cotton, and while there was something in him that wanted to curl his fist around him, touch and feel and tug and pull and be the one to bring him off, directly and deliberately, there was also no hurry to do this. Not when he was tracing patterns on his back, enjoying the gentle weight on top of him, reveling in a new sort of warmth spreading through him slowly. Enjoying the simple closeness and comfort of the rhythmic motion, the creaking of the suspension, and the song of the rain outside.

Soft kisses and soft sighs melted together after a while. Nothing louder than a whisper passed between the two men as they each tasted the sea everywhere their mouths could reach, the perfect tempo they'd fallen into not altering, not even as Gene gasped at the same feeling he got before a big wave swelled—the subtle tug at his belly button as the undercurrent was sucked away from beneath him and the way tension coiled in his arms and legs, readying to ride it out.

He could feel his orgasm rolling up on him in the distance, blood rushing through his ears like so many tons of water and the same eerie calm that always came over him at this moment, when it came to surfing or sex. The weightless clarity of the last moment before the wave crashed down on him knocked the breath out of his lungs, and he had no choice but to let it roll over him and hang on for dear life as it took him toward the shore all in a rush, tingling down his spine and spilling out of him so forcefully that he felt he had to close his eyes to survive the undeniable pleasure of the impact, only able to let his hips continue to rock gently as he came down from the high.

He waited for a sign that Dylan was approaching the same moment and watched with awe as the other man shuddered deeply, feeling him jerk his hips against him once out of time and shivering in sympathy, astounded by how beautiful he was and that he'd managed to make him feel the same way. With the same lassitude as had built up to this point, they separated, though only enough not to overheat each other. The air was still cooling, but it couldn't be said to be anything close to cold, inside or out.

Though thankful of the distance in terms of overall comfort,

Gene quickly found himself missing the contact. He groped for Dylan's hand as a reminder that this had truly just happened. Talking seemed unnecessary for long minutes, and perhaps forever, had the rain not stopped.

"Storm's over," Dylan observed quietly.

"The rain seems to be, anyway," Gene found himself agreeing, and wondering at the same time if he might turn and kiss him again, find a way to repeat what they'd just shared. He was honestly not concerned about what the weather chose to do, except as far as it was interesting to Dylan. But this was an ending, not a beginning, and he knew that treating it as such would make it easier to bear.

"Shall I take you home, then?" Strange, thinking of a room in a backpackers' hotel as anyone's home, but it was the case for so many of the people he knew here.

Dylan turned his head to face him, looking completely calm and determined in a way that hit Gene as though it was something physical. "I think I could stay here a little longer." He smiled and moved forward to kiss Gene's lips. "Long as you can put up with me."

"Oh, I think I could put up with you for a very long time." Gene grinned.

RULES IS RULES

Rob Rosen

It was a gorgeous June day in the city by the bay, the sky a dazzling blue, the sun just hot enough that you could walk the streets in nothing more than a pair of shorts and a T-shirt. And in San Francisco, in the middle of June, that's really saying something. I mean, hell, goosebumps had taken up permanent residence beneath my skin since May. In other words, I was on my motorcycle in no time flat zooming up Castro Street, the warm breeze washing over me as I headed west, the beach a-callin'.

Up, up, up I went, then down and up again, hill after crazy fucking hill, my Harley humming beneath me, cock throbbing behind the thin swatch of denim that covered it. I sighed and gave it a nudge. "Down, boy," I told it, smiling as I rounded the last bend, the top of the Golden Gate Bridge visible above the old white buildings of the Presidio.

And then I shouted "Fuck!" as I came to a grinding halt inside the nearly empty parking lot. "Fuck!" I repeated, yanking my helmet off as my body suddenly went sub-arctic. "Fucking San Francisco summers." I slumped down in my seat as I watched the fog fill in all around me, dense and white, cold as an ice chest and thick as pea soup. "Murphy's Law, one, Jeff's sunny afternoon, zero."

I hopped off my bike and popped open the small pod that held my just-in-case sweatshirt. Sadly, it got a lot of wear. Especially in June in San Francisco. And July. And a good portion of August. Then I walked over to the stairs leading down to Baker Beach. No shock there; stairs were empty. Beach, from what I could see of it, was empty, too. Empty as my head for thinking that I could lay out in June. Or July. Or the better part of August.

Still, I was there. "Maybe it'll burn off," I said to myself, rubbing my arms as I trudged down. Way down. Zigzagging my way to the fog-enshrouded beach below. And, go figure, it was even colder down there, the fog thicker, denser, and meaner than a Texas Republican. "Or maybe it won't," I glumly added. "Until fucking September."

I craned my neck left. "Deserted." Then forward, to the sound of the waves. Not the sight, though—seeing as there wasn't any—just the sound. Then up at all that fucking white. And then right, north, to what would be the gay beach. *Would* be, if anyone else was as stupid as I was to be there.

Into the fog I squinted, and, lo and behold, I could've sworn I spotted someone lying out. Or possibly frozen in place. Or maybe it was just a sea lion. Or a human-shaped rock. The only thing I knew for certain was that it wasn't a Texas Republican. Not in San Francisco, in June or otherwise. And certainly not on the northernmost tip of Baker Beach.

Still, I trudged through the sand in my sneakers, arms folded tight over my chest, bared legs confused as to why they were bare this early in the season. Them and me both. But there was something up ahead. Something pink. Something not a sea lion or a rock, though in the fog, it was mighty hard to make out exactly what in fact it was.

That is, not until I got right on up to it. Or *him*, as was the case.

"How?" I managed, teeth nearly chattering.

He pried his lids open and stared up at me, impossibly blue eyes beaming through the thick, white fog. "How," he replied, voice deep, hand held up, palm flat. "This Indian territory?" He looked around. "Where's the casino?"

I shook my head and pointed down at him, at his naked body, strangely unfrozen. "No, I meant, *how* are you lying out? And naked?"

He shrugged. "Nude beach. Rules is rules."

My head kept right on shaking as I took him in, from his bare tippy toes up his long bare body, stopping on his equally long, bare schlong, which was resting comfortably in a trimmed black bush, and then I continued to his flat tummy and hairy pecs before stopping on those eyes of blue yet again. "Um, I think *that* rule was meant to be broken. Fog trumps rule, friend."

"Ben," he informed.

I grinned. "Fog trumps rule, *Ben*," I reiterated.

He propped himself up on his elbows, pink nipples pointing up and out. It was a wonder they didn't crack and fall off, I thought, all things considered. "Fog indeed trumps rule, unless..." he said, patting the blanket beneath him.

"Magic blanket?" I hazarded. "You a genie, Ben?"

He grinned, teeth as white as the fog that continued to flow over us, nearly obliterating the beach I was no longer certain we were on. "What would your wish be if I was?" he replied, voice syrupy-sweet, tinged with something raspy and recognizable. Especially on that stretch of beach, June or otherwise.

I chuckled. "To not be so fucking cold," I told him.

"Ah," he said, sidling over a bit as he again patted the empty stretch of blanket to his side. "Your wish is my command, Master."

"Jeff," I told him.

He nodded. "Your wish is my command, Master Jeff."

The words made my cock go *boing*, temporarily thawing my winterlike mid-June chill. And so I crouched down, one hand buried in the sand, the other patting the blanket. "It's hot," I said, with a surprised chuckle. "How?"

His chuckle echoed mine, the sound crashing over me like the nearby surf over the rocks. "We've already done that routine, Jeff."

I moved in closer, both hands on the blanket now, a shock of heat pulsing up my arms. "No, I meant, how can you have a heated blanket in the middle of the beach?"

He sat up and put his hand over mine. The pulse repeated, hotter this time, tingling through my veins. "Rules is rules," he said, yet again. "And Baker Beach in June can mean only one thing."

"Fog," we both said in unison, his hand now gripping mine as I sat down next to him, the chill at last replaced by glorious warmth.

"But, again, how?" I asked, utterly at a loss.

He flipped over, alabaster ass aimed my way, hairy crack splayed as he fiddled beneath the blanket, a black box soon whipped out and up for my inspection. "Battery pack. Five hours' worth of juice in her. Just enough for a summer tan."

I stared up at the sun. Or where the sun ought to have been. If it were, say, September. Or maybe not in San Francisco on the beach. "You bring sunscreen, too?" I asked. Because, fog or no fog, five hours outside was sure to burn something fierce.

He reached his hand in front of him and grabbed for a backpack that I hadn't noticed. Then again, I could barely see a foot in front of me. Or maybe it was because my eyes were fairly glued to that stellar ass of his. I heard the zipper and then watched as he handed me the Coppertone. "Front side is done. Back side could use a schpritz."

"You're in luck," I said, grabbing the bottle as I hopped up on my knees. "I majored in schpritz."

"With a minor in Native American languages, if all that *how*ing is any indication."

He sprawled out on the heated blanket, hands digging into the sand as mine dug into his flesh, a soft moan swirling around us before it was lost in the noise of the surf. I wiped the sunscreen clear across his back, the smell of coconut wafting up my nostrils before I schpritzed even lower.

He squirmed and laughed. "Brrr. Cold."

My hands traveled further south. "Let me heat it up for you then, Ben," I said, grabbing onto his cheeks and digging in, splaying them apart as I leaned my head down for an ogle at his winking hole. I took a whiff, the smell of musk joining the heady mixture of sunscreen and salty ocean air. In for a penny, in for a pound, I darted my tongue out and gave the crinkled center a cursory lick.

"What if someone sees," he said, the chuckle returning as he spread his legs even wider apart, ass higher up, balls hanging down low.

"Doubtful," I replied, mouth on his hole now, tongue delving in. I came up for air a minute later. "I can barely see, and I'm right here." I gave his ass a playful slap, the sound echoing out in all directions.

"Ah," he said, on all fours now, legs far apart. "Good point." I spat into his hole, the saliva trickling down his swaying nuts. Then I gently worked a finger inside of him as I reached my free hand between his thighs, my hand gripping his hard-as-granite pole, which throbbed as I gave it a tug and a stroke. "Here's another good point, Ben," I said.

"Feels more like two," he said, moaning as he bucked his ass into my hand.

"Three," I admitted. "But who's counting?" In fact, all three spit-slick fingers were now buried deep inside his ass. But that wasn't the point in question. "No, my point was that I'm on a nude beach and I'm not nude."

"And rules is rules," he reminded me.

"Only, you're on the hot blanket, and I'd be up here in the frigid cold. And a polar woody sounds awfully painful." I laughed as I added, "Gives a whole new meaning to the term blue balls."

He crawled forward, his ass retracting from my fingers in an audible *pop*. Then he jumped up and motioned for me to do the same. So I too jumped and then stood in front of him as he reached down and then promptly wrapped the blanket around the both of us, the warmth returning as his eyes met mine, his so blue that they put the sky to shame. What little of it there was to see, that is. "Better?" he asked, his lips brushing mine as a swarm of butterflies got loose inside my belly.

"Much," I exhaled, my lips grinding into his, the chill obliterated as the blanket covered us up, his cock poking my belly. "Almost," I amended, realizing my own cock was still encased in denim. Then I reached down, grabbed the bottom of my t-shirt and hiked it up and off. "Closer," I added.

He rubbed his free hand across my chest, the other holding the blanket as he pinched my nipple and gave it a tweak. My eyelids fluttered, a groan traveling up from my lungs. Still, I had work to do. And *closer* wasn't quite there. Meaning, the denim shorts dropped to the sand, tighty-whities all the tighter with my cock filling up every square inch of cotton. And then, quick as a wink, I was nude on the nude beach, tree limb of a prick at last free, jutting out to meet its newfound friend. Needless to say, no *down, boy* this go-round.

"About time," he whispered into my mouth, eyes an inch from mine, his body again pressed up tight as the blanket encased us, heat cycloning around me even as the fog grew ever thicker, like we were lost in a cloud.

I reached my hands around his waist and again cupped his ass, fingers delving dead-center, pushing and prodding against his still-wet hole. "Now, where were we?" I rasped in his ear, taking a tender lobe in between my teeth for a gnash and a chew.

He moaned and shivered into me. "I believe we were at three good points." He reached down and grabbed my cock, a million volts of adrenaline suddenly surging through me. "But I'd settle for one really big one."

"Settle for or settle *on*?" I asked, one hand reaching in front of him to grab his massive tool, the head already slick. I wiped the salty jizz off and sucked my index finger clean.

"You always talk this dirty to guys you've just met on deserted nude beaches?" he asked, a question for a question.

"Rules is rules."

"So they say," he retorted, bending down again, backpack unzipped, a square flash of foil and a bottle of something slick happily glimpsed through the dense fog. Then he grabbed my hand and began walking me up the beach, ever northward as our cocks swayed in rhythm. "So they say."

Thankfully, we still had our sneakers on. That and the blanket and permafrozen smiles on our faces. Needless to say, even with the fog that was still zooming past, I could see that we were alone out there. No-man's land. Or make that two-man's land. Our-man's land. Me and Ben, the sand and the surf, and the occasional piece of driftwood or stone outcrop to keep us company.

We made our way closer to the shoreline, the waves crashing directly in front of us. I could just make them out, with the cold Pacific lapping at our feet, eager for someone, anyone, to come and play with it. "Please tell me we're not going for a swim, Ben," I said, hand in his hand, cock pointing dead ahead. "I don't think the blanket would keep us warm in there for very long."

"Not there," he replied, pointing instead to a large brown form a few feet away. "There."

I squinted into the fog, the rock taking shape as we drew nearer. "All the comforts of home," I quipped, hopping on, the blanket warm beneath my ass and against my back. And then I wrapped it around me and over him as he sank to his knees into the sand. Or, more importantly, sank his mouth into my crotch. I breathed in, deeply, the smell of ocean filling up my sinus cavity as my cock filled up his oral one. "Mmm," I groaned, the Pacific groaning right on back at me.

He popped my prick out and slapped the fat, glistening head against his full lips before glancing up at me, those eyes sparkling like sapphires. "Hot time, summer in the city," he semi-sang.

I ran my hand through his tangle of jet-black hair. "Battery-packed though that hot might be."

He giggled and stood up, lips again meshed with mine, tongues doing a midair tango as I heard the foil tearing open, the sound sending a spark down my spine that made my cock twitch. I watched him slide the rubber over my prick, the lube quickly dripping down my sheathed-up shaft. I grabbed the bottle as he turned around, my hand in his crack, fingers, plural, quickly gliding inside of him, thick gobs of Wet sloshing up and in.

And then he backed up, my hand again free as he positioned his stunning ass just above my pole. Round peg, round hole, perfect fit. Down he sank as my cock slid in, the blanket wrapped around us, heat on the outside, heat on the inside. I nibbled on his neck as he sank even lower, until he was grinding his ass into my dick, mashing my balls with his cheeks, groaning so loudly that I could no longer hear the surf.

I reached around and grabbed his dick. His body quaked as I gave it a stroke, the sweat on his back gluing my front to him, until it was impossible to tell where he ended and I began. A seagull flew overhead, squawking at our shenanigans. Or perhaps it was just jealous that someone was keeping warm on a beach day in June in San Francisco.

Up and down his ass went on my cock, each time getting a moan from me, a groan from him, my palm working faster and faster on his prick. "Close," he soon howled into the fog, the sound booming all around as it bounced off the cliffs behind us.

I shoved my dick as deep as it would go and pounded his rod fast as lightning. His head tilted back, sweat flinging off of him as his cock grew surprisingly thicker in my hand. And then he spewed, thick bands of cum flying this way and that before landing noiselessly in the sand. A split second later, his ring gripping my prick, I filled up that rubber with a load so big that my entire protein reservoir was wiped clean out.

I panted as I jerked every last drop of spunk out from his dick while he ground his ass into me and did the same with mine, until we were both spent and soaked with sweat. Slowly, he stood up, my cock springing free, the rubber quickly buried in the sand for posterity's sake. Then he grabbed my hand and walked me to our starting place, the backpack where we'd left it, the blanket again spread out, me spooning him as we drifted off into wave-crashing slumber.

When I woke up, Lord knows how much later, the fog had lifted, the beach pristine, the magnificent orange bridge looming high overhead as the Pacific rolled in far below her golden gates. I sat up and looked around. Not too surprisingly, we were no longer alone, other nude men, other blankets, joining us on our remote patch of paradise.

Ben stretched and yawned and also sat up, then stared at me with those stunning eyes of his. "Neat," he said, with a wide grin. "You're even better looking in the light of day."

I ran my finger down his stubbled, tanned cheek. "Ditto."

Then he leaned in, his lips finding mine, warm as, well, the sand beneath us. Finally. And again those butterflies took wing inside my belly, my cock stirring as his tongue swirled around my own.

Down, boy, I willed it.

Though, of course, it was already too late.

Because, as they say, rules is rules. Especially on a nude beach in San Francisco. Even in June.

WHAT WASHED ASHORE

D. K. Jernigan

A sharp bark near my head dragged me out of the sea of oblivion, and I lay moaning on the shores of consciousness as the pain in my face and body came rushing back. A wet snuffling at my ear reminded me of the proximity of the dog, and I reached up a shaky arm to tangle my fingers in silky fur. "Hey doggy," I said. My voice was slurred and thick, and I realized I was speaking through a split lip. I moaned again, still not daring to open my eyes. Had my head been injured? There was a rushing sound in my ears, rising and falling in a constant rhythm.

The dog started to lick my face, and then suddenly he was gone and a deep, masculine voice startled me. The dog's owner, I guessed. "Hey man, you okay? Need me to call anyone?"

I jerked, which set off bursts of pain throughout my body, and I moaned again, feeling like the world's biggest crybaby. "I feel like I got hit by a truck," I said. The image of five men standing around me, laughing and kicking, pushed its way to the fore and I did my best to shove it back. The sound of a seabird brought me back to the present, and suddenly the rushing sound made sense. "Holy shit, is that the ocean?"

"Well, you did sort of pass out on the beach," the voice said. "Look, do you need me to call an ambulance or a girlfriend or someone?"

How the hell did I get to the beach? "Where am I?" My head was throbbing. I raised my hands to my eyes, but the pressure brought a screaming pain and I dropped them again. Damn.

"Seabright," the man answered, and when that didn't get a response, "Near the Boardwalk?"

"The Boardwalk? Like in Santa Cruz?" *Those assholes dragged me all the way to Santa Cruz?*

"Okay, yeah, I'm going to just let you sleep it off, man. No worries, okay?"

I snorted painfully. "I'm not drunk. The last thing I remember was walking out of Spla—um, a bar. In San Jose." Splash was a gay bar and dance club over the hill, and the last thing I needed was to incite a second gay bashing in two days. Santa Cruz was known for being sort of hippie, but why take the chance?

"You're from over the hill? Who the fuck did you piss off?" The man's voice had been drawing away, but he'd returned and was standing over me now.

"Suffice it to say, it wasn't anything I did wrong." I cracked my eyes open and when that didn't kill me, I rolled slightly to one side and moaned as I tried to push up to a seated position.

"Shit." The man hesitated. "You clean?"

"I just told you I'm not drunk," I said, concentrating on trying to keep my arms under me.

"No, but you're covered in blood. You contagious?"

"Oh, yes. I mean, no. God! I mean I'm clean. And I'm Cam, by the way. Thanks for stopping."

"Yeah. I'm Bryant." I looked up to greet my rescuer and had to refrain from drooling, even with my throbbing body eager to distract me. The guy wore sweats like some men wear designer suits, with shoulders that screamed for attention even through the thick fabric. His hair was just long enough to look sexy and tousled, and his eyes were the same gray-green as the sea beyond him. I wobbled a little, and he ducked to take my arm and steady me. "Take it easy," he urged, but I just shook my head. I needed to get up before I could process how much it was going to hurt to do all that moving.

"I'm okay." I winced as he helped me climb to my feet. My entire body would be covered in bruises from five pairs of feet kicking and stomping. I stepped forward, testing myself, and my leg buckled under me. Bryant moved quickly and managed to hook me by the armpit, keeping me upright.

"Shit. I'm sorry." *How humiliating. I'm on a beach with the cutest guy I've met in months, and I can't even stand up by myself.* And with that, the rest of my awareness came back completely. I was damp and fucking freezing in a thin cotton shirt and jeans. My body began to tremble wildly, and Bryant had to wrap his arm around my waist and grip my arm where it draped over his shoulder to keep me steady. His large ball of golden fur jumped around at our feet, barking and whining.

Bryant heaved a put-out sigh, and then almost reluctantly gestured up toward the street. "I have a car that isn't too far away. I can get the heater turned on for you. Come on, you can do it."

Step by step he practically carried me up the beach, pausing when I tripped in the heavy sand, patiently steadying me and nearly dragging me until we got to a strip of dirt, then sidewalk. "Just up there," he said, gesturing to a car parked nearby. "Come on, Jack!" Jack, the dog, left off whatever he was sniffing and bounded over to us, following obediently as his master and his beach find climbed the slight hill to a blue Jetta. Bryant unlocked the doors and slid my sandy, bloody self into the passenger seat.

I exhaled a small moan of relief to be off my feet and took a deep, steadying breath. With my eyes pressed shut I listened as first one door opened behind me—presumably to admit Jack— and then a moment later the driver's door opened and the car settled as he slid in. It wasn't long before the engine had warmed up and I could bask in the heat, taking the worst of the chill out of my bones. Behind me, Jack licked at my ear in what I assumed was sympathy.

"So, uh, do you have someone I can call?" Bryant asked.

I looked over to see him flashing a cell phone at me as if I wouldn't know what he meant.

I sighed. "Not really. I moved out here last month to be with my—with the person I was seeing. But things didn't exactly work out." That was putting it mildly. "I've been looking for a job, but I don't have anything yet. No family, no friends..."

"Maybe I should just take you to the hospital, then."

"No health insurance." He looked resigned, and I felt bad for the guy. He certainly didn't ask to be stuck with some random guy bleeding in his car. "If I could just have a few more minutes with your lovely heater, you can leave me here and I'll call a cab."

"Your buddies left you with your wallet?"

Fuck. I shifted my weight and realized that my back pockets were empty. I moaned, and this time when he spoke he sounded sympathetic. "Look, I have to get ready for work. You can come back to my place and get cleaned up and have a nap or some-thing, and when I get off I can take you back to wherever you belong, okay?"

"I don't know..." It was incredibly generous, and I suddenly felt guilty thinking of how much I'd probably inconvenienced him already. *God, I hope I'm not bleeding on his seats.*

"It's either that or I drop you off at the police station, where they'll probably insist on the hospital and the fifth degree about what you remember. I mean, I can do that, too, if you prefer."

"Shit. I guess... thank you."

"Alrighty then." The car pulled away from the curb, and that was the last thing I knew until Bryant gently shook me awake in front of his apartment.

I climbed out of the car on my own and even though it hurt like hell, I could walk by myself again, thank goodness. Bryant unlocked the door and as I followed him in, Jack made a beeline for a filthy blanket on the couch, which he playfully savaged for a minute before sprawling out across it. "Um, so, I need to shower and get to work. TV's there, there's some snacks in that cupboard you can eat if you're hungry. Or whatever's in the fridge, but I don't cook much. I should be back by like five."

Bryant disappeared into the bathroom, and I sat down heavily on the couch. Jack immediately flopped over toward me, laying his head in my lap in an obvious ploy for a good scratching. "Hey, buddy," I said, obliging him. His fur was like silk, and I sighed in pleasure as I ran my fingers through it. I must have dozed off again, because it felt like only seconds later that the bathroom door swung open. I tried to keep my eyes on the floor, but I couldn't help peeking as Bryant emerged wearing nothing but a towel and looking as delicious as I could have hoped for.

His shoulders were just as muscled and perfect as I'd guessed, but even I couldn't have dared dream of the chiseled chest and the delicate curves of his abs with just a dusting of dark hair leading down under the towel. I shifted uncomfortably and leaned forward to try to hide the bulge that had appeared like magic in my jeans—it was, remarkably, the only place I didn't feel like I'd been kicked last night.

By the time he reappeared with clothing on, I'd gotten a firm grip on myself and was hopeful I could make it through the encounter without embarrassing myself. "Thank you for letting me wait here," I said as he came back.

"It's cool," he said, shrugging uncomfortably. He crossed to the kitchen and grabbed an energy bar before turning back to study me. "You really look like shit. Feel free to use the bathroom and get yourself cleaned up. I put out some clothes in my room that should fit you if you want to change." He paused. "I was going to say you could sleep on the couch, but you might have to wrestle the dog."

"I'll be fine," I said, but he was already shaking his head.

"I've seen you doze off twice already. You can take the bed. Just do me a favor and wash the blood and sand off first." He smiled then, and I nearly embarrassed myself again. My pulse couldn't help but react to the way it warmed and softened his entire face. Fortunately for me, he glanced at a clock on the wall, swore softly, and produced a bike from behind the couch. "I'm off. Back soon. You can knock at the door downstairs if you need anything – Anita's pretty cool."

As the door shut behind him, I turned and faced Jack, who was looking up at me with huge, liquid eyes. "Guess I should check out that shower, huh?"

My face startled me when I first caught sight of it in the mirror. The lower half of my face was smeared with blood from where an early punch had caught me across the nose, and my lower lip was split and fat. A fat bruise colored my temple—I assumed that was the one that had finally put my lights out—but my nose was still strong and straight, unbroken, and somehow my dark blue eyes remained unblackened. My body, as I peeled my clothes off, was colorful with bruises. My muscular frame was looking a little worse for wear, but I was aware that things could have been much worse.

The hot water felt wonderful, and within a few minutes I felt good enough to start remembering the way Bryant had looked, wet and sexy and muscular as he came out of this very bathroom. I closed my eyes and my breath deepened as I let my imagination run away with me a little. My hand closed around the base of my cock and began to stroke softly as I pictured him stopping in the doorway, his eyes narrowed with lust as that beautiful smile crinkled his eyes.

I gave a little squeeze and twist as I imagined him dropping the towel. My cock throbbed in my hand as I pictured how the rest of his body would look, his own cock hard and ready as it was exposed. In my mind I stood and crossed the room, and my moan filled the shower as I pictured myself kissing him. As our tongues danced together in my mind, my body trembled with pleasure and excitement and my hand sped up on my cock.

I groaned with pleasure as I imagined Bryant dropping to his knees and pulling my shorts gently down around my ankles. My cock sprang free and he gazed up at me, his grin playful now. His hands traced up the insides of my legs, avoiding the ultimate destination as he laughed and teased and played with me, his eyes never leaving my face as I began to moan and quiver.

"God, yes," I whispered, and I imagined the way Bryant would smile back at me and lick his lips before reaching out, oh so slowly, to touch his tongue to the tip of my cock. I threw my head back and moaned, and felt his playful licks turn serious as his mouth closed around the head of my cock. He sucked gently, taking more of me into himself, and I groaned again, my fist pumping faster in real life as I pictured Bryant picking up speed, bobbing up and down over my erection as I brushed my hands over his face and hair and thrust back into his mouth. As I watched him, his eyes flew open and the look of lust I pictured on his face was enough to send me right over the edge.

My eyes flew open as I came, moaning loudly and nearly doubling up at the pleasure that pulsed through me. *Holy shit, that was hot!* It was probably rude to masturbate in the shower of the guy who had saved me from freezing my unconscious ass off on the beach, but he was the hottest guy I'd seen half-naked in years.

Feeling sheepish about my fantasizing, I finished scrubbing off and grabbed a fresh towel to go in search of the clothes he'd set out for me. They looked like a good fit, which was surprising since he was taller and a little thinner than me, but I put on the underwear and T-shirt, set the pants aside, and crawled into his bed to let my body rest and heal. I drifted off to sleep with the erotic scent of him surrounding me.

"Cam?" The voice sounded like it was coming from miles away. I rolled toward it, my eyes still shut. Something smelled so… *good*. I inhaled deeply and felt a hand on my arm. "Hey, Cam."

My cock had quickly hardened at the smell and the sensation of soft sheets and that sexy, familiar voice. "Hey, baby," I said, pushing back the covers to reveal my rock-hard reaction. I heard a gasp and the fog I was in cleared. *Oh, fuck.* My eyes flew open and I pulled at the covers at the same time.

Bryant was standing over the bed, his eyes wide and his mouth open, but the expression wasn't the disgust I had expected. As I puzzled over that, a motion at the corner of my eye caught my attention and I glanced down to track it. Bryant's cock twitched against his slacks again, and my own eyes widened.

"I'm sorry," Bryant said, misunderstanding my expression. He started to back away.

"I'm not," I blurted out. Bryant froze, and the precise lustful look that had set me on fire in my imagination flared to life in his eyes.

"I don't want to take advantage," he started, and I sat up in the bed, letting the covers fall away.

"Do you want me to leave?"

"Not really, no," he said on a strangled chuckle. I pulled his T-shirt up over my head, and Bryant leaned toward me as if pulled by an invisible string. I reached out hesitantly and rested my hand on his hip, and Bryant moved as if a dam had broken inside him, whipping off his own shirt and flowing forward to straddle me on the bed, pressing me back into the pillows.

"There's just one thing," I whispered, reaching up to cup my hand behind his head. He raised his brows inquisitively and I grinned. "I like to be on top," I said, rolling him with me so that I knelt over him in a tangle of bedding. I felt the move jostle and stretch my bruised muscles, but when my eyes narrowed it was as much from lust as from pain.

"Oh *God*," he moaned. He arched up toward me and I delighted in the wild lust that teased over his features.

"You okay with that?" I asked, lowering my face over his.

He reached up and kissed me in answer, letting his tongue play over mine for a moment before I took control of the kiss. We stayed frozen just like that for several long moments, only our tongues moving, teasing over one another, before I curled my fingers in his sun-kissed hair and pulled his head back to bare his neck. As I moved down his body to lick and nibble at the tender, exposed flesh, he gave a whimper of pleasure and shifted his hips to rub his rock-solid erection against me.

"That's hot," I whispered in his ear, and my hot breath made him buck again and reach for my cock. I eased back to shuck the borrowed underwear and he watched, eyeing me hungrily. "I look like a rainbow," I joked, gesturing at the bruises across my torso. I was trying to ignore the throbbing along my ribs.

"Bruises aside, you look like a wet dream come to life. If I took every surfer I'd ever ogled and rolled them into one, you'd still probably be hotter," he murmured back, and I smiled as his hand went to his own cock, straining against his pants.

I grinned back down at him and wrapped my hand around my cock for the second time that day, making sure to give my arms a little more flex than necessary. "This isn't the first time today I've touched myself while picturing you naked," I told him. He moaned and my grin widened. "You want to hear about it?"

"Tell me," he gasped, bucking his hips up as he rubbed himself through his slacks. His eyes were on my thick cock, hungry and a little wild. *Fuck*, was he hot.

"I saw you coming out of the bathroom today, all wet and sexy," I said, letting my head fall back as I stroked myself a little harder. "I thought you were straight, but I stood in your shower and imagined you anyway. I pictured you on your knees sucking me off." His loud moan interrupted me, and I brought my attention back to his flushed face. "You like that?" He nodded, panting. "You want to suck my cock, Bryant?"

He sat up slowly, looking hungry, and moved off the bed without taking his eyes off me. "I don't mind being on top if that's what a guy wants, but I've been waiting a long time for a man who would push me down on the bed and fuck me until I scream," he said.

My split lip was killing me, but my grin only got bigger as I turned so that I was sitting on the edge of the bed. "We'll get to that," I said, and with a moan that made my cock twitch, Bryant dropped to his knees in front of me and in one smooth move took my entire cock in his mouth. "Holy *shit*," I said, throwing my head back as he swallowed me. When I glanced back down, his eyes were sparkling with pleasure as he knelt there, my cock buried in his throat and his face nestled among my pubes. His throat worked around me for another few seconds before he pulled back slowly and then, just as slowly, swallowed me again. He hummed in pleasure and the vibrations carried straight to the base of my spine.

"I want to fuck your face, Bryant. How do you feel about that?" He moaned again, and I answered with a groan of my own before I stood up, edging him back, and ran my fingers through his hair. "You are one sexy fucking man," I said, pressing on the back of his head to force my cock as far down his throat as humanly possible. He hummed his satisfaction as I rocked from side to side for a few seconds, then I pulled slowly back, feeling his tongue playing over the underside of my cock as I moved.

My hand tightened to grip his hair, and with a grunt of exquisite satisfaction I rocked my hips back and then deep into his hot, tight throat. My sore muscles protested, but it was easy to ignore them when his throat tightened and my balls sent a jolt of pleasure through me. His lips, tongue, and throat played skillfully over me as I picked up the pace, fucking his face faster and harder, slamming deep into his throat again and again until the pleasure building in my balls was almost too much to stand. Then I pulled away from him and smiled at Bryant's disappointed little mew.

"I want to suck you dry," he said, reaching for me again, but I held him back.

"I thought you wanted me to fuck you until you screamed," I reminded him, and he moaned and reached for the bulge in his slacks again. "Mmm, that's really hot, you kneeling there fondling yourself like that."

"What can I say, Cam? You're inspiring," he said, continuing the stroke himself through his pants, reaching down occasionally to cup his balls or reaching up with his other hand to rub the back of his neck or tweak his own nipples. I resisted the temptation to stroke myself while I watched him—I wanted to be able to last when I started pounding into his ass. I almost needed to pinch myself to be sure I wasn't dreaming.

As I watched him, I reached over to the nightstand and opened the top drawer, glad to see a supply of condoms and a bottle of lube. I tore off a condom packet and placed it on the night table with the lube before I reached down and helped Bryant to his feet and out of his slacks. His cock was beautiful, almost pink compared to the lightly tanned rest of him, and long and slender without being too thin—much like the man himself.

"On your knees," I said quietly, and Bryant moved quickly into position as I slicked up a couple of my fingers. The dark red rosebud of his asshole clenched and released, practically begging for attention, and I moaned as I parted his cheeks and teased at it with the tip of one finger. He pushed back at me, and I laughed and teased for a few seconds more before slipping one finger inside him, fucking him slowly as he clenched desperately around me and moaned into the pillow. "More?"

"Please!" he shouted. I smiled around my split lip and slid a second finger into him, pumping only a couple of times before I stretched him even wider with a third finger. "Oh, yes. Cam, that's so good." I continued to finger him with a steady rhythm as I reached for the condom with my free hand, tore the package with my teeth, and managed to slip it on without breaking rhythm.

In one smooth move I pulled my fingers free, positioned the

head of my cock at his hungry hole, and thrust home, driving myself deep inside him. Cam screamed and cried "Yes, fuck, yes," into his pillow as I penetrated him. I gave him only a minute to acclimate, then with one hand on his shoulder and one on his hip I pulled back and thrust deep, pounding into him while trying to avoid slamming any of my bruised flesh against his body. He moved one hand to his cock and I moaned as he started to jerk himself off while I slammed into him, hard.

It was a surprisingly short time before he cried out again and I felt his body pulse around my cock as he came. "That's right, baby, give it to me," I moaned, and my tempo took on a new urgency as I slammed into him again and again, holding off as long as I could to enjoy his wild screams and howls into the bedding. When I couldn't hold back one more second I buried myself deep and threw my head back to bask in the ecstasy that washed over me, starting at my balls and pulsing in waves through my entire body. For a minute, anyway, I felt good as new.

It was several moments of panting, tangled around one another, before I felt strong enough to get up and get rid of the condom. "I'll take you wherever you want to go," Bryant said when I got back, "but I hope you'll at least consider staying the night. I jog that beach every morning, but I've got to say, Cam, you're the best beach find I've ever made."

TANIWHA

Emily Veinglory

John Henderson let the river current carry his kayak gently down the center of the wide brown river. He rested the double-ended paddle in front of him and leaned back. With his left hand he reached up to the large, roughly oblong pendant that hung around his neck. His stepmother had given it to him just that morning.

"You be careful on the river, *Hone*," she'd said.

"John," he corrected quietly. He never accepted how she used the Maori version of his name. You had to go five generations back to find Maori blood in his family tree and he hadn't exactly been raised in the culture. "Just plain John."

"You take this, boy," she said as she placed the smooth stone in his hand. "Make sure you don't anger the *taniwha*." She looked in his eyes. "You don't want to anger the taniwha, or anyone he claims as his own."

John was always uncomfortable around Aroha. His dad had shacked up with her just after John left for university and married her a year later. Their second wedding anniversary had just passed, but John knew he still felt closer to the memory of his prim but doting mother than the very-much-alive Aroha Henderson, who included him effortlessly but haphazardly into her notion of family.

John had felt the age in the stone immediately. Its shape was reminiscent of a tongue or a *tiaha* blade, and a faint face was etched in its tip. Aroha had reached up and tied the plaited cord around his neck, her warm breasts uncomfortably close to his face. John blushed as he backed away. He wasn't sure exactly what the stone was, and whether he was being given it to hold or to keep. Either way he'd just wanted to be out on the river and away from all of... this.

An old mate from school had given him a lift upstream on the way out to the beach. The plastic kayak, Old Yella, had rattled around on the roof of his Datsun, tied down by long bungee ropes that hooked into the rolled-down windows. Now he could just take things easy, drifting home downstream. Well, not *home* exactly. Not anymore.

The current kept the kayak near the center of the river. It had been raining up in the hills and the water was cloudy and running high. But in broad blue sky the bright sun beamed down on him. John arched his back and tried to relax; that was the point of this visit, after all. He had sat his final exams and had a few weeks to unwind before starting his master's program.

John took off his T-shirt, just to feel the air on his skin. His physique was passable at best, not bulging with muscle, but lean and symmetrical like a swimmer; his skin was pale from a year spent more in study than in nature. But his body seemed to remember the long slow strokes of the paddle; it seemed to remember the river.

After a few deep breaths he felt some sense of perspective

returning. Had his mistake been in coming home? Perhaps he was some kind of latent bigot and that was really his problem with Aroha. Or was he sulking like some child that his father had gone on with his life after Mum had died? It was hard to know; neither of his parents had set him up well for under-standing emotions. Emotions were to be immediately expressed (Dad) or eternally suppressed (Mum), and that was all.

But he was an adult now. He could do whatever the hell he wanted. And one of the things he had to do was finally *tell* his Dad, before the secret and the silence became a permanent barrier between them. He'd had three years at Uni to get over the awkwardness and accept himself. Getting through whatever his father would say was probably going to be harder.

John coasted into an area of farmland. With no trees at the waterline, the landscape opened up bright and green around him. The bank had slipped a bit; a new bend was forming where the river wriggled in the grip of the pastoral landscape. Restrained, but not tamed. John dug the paddle in and pulled toward the far shore.

There was a small muddy beach and the plastic bottom of the kayak scraped up onto it. John stepped out; the water was warm around his ankles. There were geothermal hot spots all along the river here. John dragged his kayak a bit further up. Wading back out into the water, he felt the warm, slimy silt swirl around his ankles even as the chilly flow of the water eddied up over his knees and thighs. He had meant to stop around here for lunch, but his sandwich stayed in the kayak. Somehow it was the river that continued to draw him—and a hunger that was not so easily sated. He just stood thigh-deep in the water, trying to decide what to do.

But he did want to delay, to stop a while before slipping down the river back to the house. Dad thought John had a problem with

Aroha being young, being nearer John's own age. He thought John fancied her; it clearly fed his pride that he had a pretty young wife and John... well, John was not often seen with girls. John sighed. He wished he didn't care what his father thought.

He felt a slick tendril slide along his inner thigh.

Bloody hell, son of a— "Just an eel," he assured himself as he flailed back two steps. He froze. *Just an eel.*

He edged towards the shore. Then the kayak bobbed out from under his hands and started to float slowly away from him. Part of him knew there was no way it could have moved the way it did on the sluggish river. He splashed forward but the kayak was already getting away into the deeper water. John lurched after it, feeling the cold water soak through the groin of his shorts and then lapping over the waistband. He leapt forward and grabbed the scarred plastic deck just before it escaped, fingers scrabbling until he got a good hold on the rim of the storage hatch in the stern.

"Aha, got you, you bastard."

The riverbank slipped away from beneath his feet but John felt secure enough, so long as he had a grip on the kayak. He made his way, hand over hand, and turned it perpendicular to the current. He was just about to lift himself up into the cockpit when he felt something grab his trailing left ankle.

It was an unmistakable feeling. It was not a submerged log, a strand of weed or lost anchor roper—it was a hand. John kicked hard, as hard as he dared without swamping the kayak. The hand held him implacably. Adrenaline washed through him, fizzing like dry ice. His mind groped for plausible scenarios. Could it be a prankster in scuba gear? Not even in the deepest waters of a river. He tried easing his foot upwards, but the hand only tightened its grip and pulled downward.

John experienced a cascade of clichés: He thought of his family and his life. His bladder released and his whole body began to shake. He was vaguely intrigued by the fact that fear did indeed have these literal effects. He also realized that his unadventurous life had given him very little to remember or regret.

Another hand closed over his left calf. The downward pull strengthened; the kayak trembled and sank lower so that the water began to stream over its slender prow.

He regretted not telling his Dad, not trying a bit harder with Aroha—she hadn't done anything wrong....

John felt a strange paralysis as he sank slowly in the water. It seemed even colder. John's fingers made a vain squeaking sound as they slipped over the hard carapace of the kayak. His forearms felt weak. He realized dimly that he was very much going out with a whimper.

The hands suddenly released their grip; John bobbed in the water. With a gasp he was torn between wanting to get out of the water and wanting to turn and face the threat. John craned to look down into the milky depths. He could see the greenstone hanging from his neck—the tip of its tonguelike form just brushing the water. The murky shape of a three-fingered hand emerged slowly from the dark current.

With a swift jerk the dark hand grabbed him again and pulled him under the water, down through the swift currents into the cold, cold, deep darkness.

He awoke, but into a dream. Or at least it seemed like a dream. John could feel that he was breathing, but at the same time he was underwater. He floated upright, arms flung out. He was still being pulled down, but slowly, and then he just hung in the murky water. Then he was still. Even the current had vanished. He was perfectly weightless, staring into the veils of coffee-colored water, the heart of the river.

He looked down again, just able to make out a dark shape, still feeling the hand holding his ankle like an anchor, like a band. Whoever, whatever it was moved, then rose very slowly through the water.

It was a person, yes, a man. But not quite. Its right hand curled just behind John's knee as it—no, he—floated languorously upward. Then the man from the depths looked up. Human—mostly. His eyes glowed the metallic green-blue of a *paua* shell. His mouth was wide and parted to offer a glimpse of sharp, pointed teeth. And again the three-fingered hand, releasing John's ankle and reaching up in an effortless, swooping motion to the band of his shorts.

Taniwha.

Of course he'd heard of the mythical taniwha, the river monster, something to scare kids with and keep them away from the river. He was vaguely aware there was more to the story, about the taniwha being symbolic of the power of the chief, about there being one for every bend of the river. But he'd never known anyone who seriously thought they could be real.

Except maybe Aroha.

The taniwha pulled John's shorts down and off. John watched them drift away and swiftly vanish into the murk. He felt rather than saw when the taniwha took his cock in its mouth. Cold shock, John's eyes opened wide, and he looked down to a mass of swirling green-black hair against his pallid groin.

This must be a dream.

It felt warm. Sucking, rasping. He felt the light brushing of those dozens of tiny teeth. A threat or a promise that threw the animal response building up inside him into stark contrast. He didn't look down again. That made it seem too real. He looked ahead into the water, a mass of motes and tiny bubbles that seemed to pulse in time with the beating of his heart.

The creature sucked him, slow and long, then swallowed him deep. Each time, the tiny teeth touched his cock right at the base in a tidy ring. They seemed to say: so easy. So easy to shear this right off and make a meal of it. Make an end of you, right here. At first John felt a pulse of fear at each embrace of those tiny teeth. A deep beat of his head echoed out like a drum. The pendant on his chest jumped on his suddenly tender, resonating skin. The water flinched and swayed.

But each time it happened his fear faded a bit, until it entirely faded away.

He was in the hands of something older, something more powerful than any force against which struggle would make sense. He would be maimed, killed, or delivered to safety at the whim of the taniwha, and he had to be at peace with that. It was surprisingly easy. The tickle of teeth became part of the pleasure. Each fate came to feel somewhat the same, so that if he even had been given a choice, he would have been indifferent.

Then there was only the touch. Eyes closed. Two hands holding him. The tongue, rough as a cat's. The mouth, wide as a shark's. The teeth, tickling. The climax dark, drowning, and welcome.

An ambiguous space, of place and mind, resolved slowly into the riverbank at night. He was wearing his shorts and T-shirt again, barely even wet. Old Yella was pulled up neatly on the bank beside him with the paddle sticking up out of the cockpit. He recognized the pilings she was tucked up against as the old jetty next to the rainwater culvert, just one bend of the river away from his father's house.

Checking with one hand John found himself... intact. Well, physically, at least.

There was some appeal to the idea of just pulling the kayak

up into the bushes and walking the rest of the way home. Or running.

But he had begun this journey in the water, and it seemed only fitting to end it the same way. In the end he had not been afraid. Not then, so why now? He wasn't ready to think about it. He suspected he'd be thinking about it on and off for the rest of his life, so there was no hurry to get started.

He yanked the grab handle and skated the kayak back onto the river, and then settled into the seat and guided himself cautiously down the last stretch. The water ran swift at night because that was when they opened the dam sluice if there had been rain up in the hills. There was just enough light to see, from the stars and from the windows of a few distant houses blinking between the trees.

He came up all too quickly on the little clay bank nearest Dad's place and dragged the kayak up under the trees, securing the stern with a bungee cord before walking up toward the house though the quiet streets. This far out of town there was just a streetlight on each corner, with reservoirs of darkness in between.

He let himself in through the back door. Aroha was in the kitchen unloading the dishwasher. She took one look at him and seemed to see it all. See it all and have nothing much to say about it.

His father came through from the living room in a burst. "Where on earth have you been?" he snapped. "It shouldn't have taken you this long to get down from the Schmitt place. If you were going to start further up you should have said. It's for safety, you know. So we know where to look for you if you don't come back. And besides, you shouldn't have gone so far that it would be dark before you got back."

John shrugged. "I started at the Schmitt farm. This is just how long the river took to get me back."

"That's impossible."

Aroha came around them on her way to the living room. "Maybe the river had something to show him."

John could see that his dad didn't agree with this philosophical perspective, but didn't want to be disrespectful of Aroha's point of view. He just clenched his jaw and looked for another target.

"What the hell is that?" His eyes settled on the heavy pendant hanging down from John's neck.

"Oh, right." John reached up, expecting to struggle with the knotted linen cord, but it came free easily in his hands. "Just something Aroha lent me."

"What do you mean?" his father barked. "That's clearly a museum-qua—"

John walked past his father and passed the greenstone pendant back to Aroha, who was now sitting on the sofa flipping through the *Listener* as if she didn't have a care in the world. Whatever the stone was, it wasn't anything he could or would explain. He was glad to be rid of it.

"Did the river have something to show you?" she asked quietly.

"Yeah, I think it did."

"What are you two whispering about?" He could see his father's suspicions flaring up. But perhaps for the first time he was considering not only that John fancied Aroha, but that Aroha might fancy him back. It was going to be easy to set that right. And Aroha's presence suddenly became strangely reassuring. Because the two of them knew that there are things in life so much more important than sexual orientation and worrying about winning or losing the approval of your father.

"Hey, Dad," John said. "Come sit down. There's something I need to tell you."

ISLAND
GETAWAY

Neil Plakcy

I f you're not happy here, there's the door." Mike pointed toward the front door, where our golden retriever, Roby, sat nervously watching us argue.

"You're such a drama queen," I said. "Just because I don't like the way you throw your clothes around the house doesn't mean I want to move out."

We stood there facing each other. At just over six-four, Mike is about three inches taller than I am, though we both have straight dark hair, and because we're both mixed-race we both have a slight epicanthic fold over our eyes. My skin is darker than his, but not by much, and sometimes people think that we're brothers or cousins rather than partners.

"I don't know, Kimo, it seems like all we do is argue lately. We're both always working, and when we get home we just get on each other's nerves."

I couldn't disagree with that—but I wasn't ready to give up on the two years we'd spent living together, or the magnetic connection I felt to him when things were good.

"So what do we do?" I asked. "You want to talk to a counselor or someone?"

"I don't think that kind of thing works. And I don't like the idea of somebody else getting into our business."

At least he was still using the plural pronoun. He sat down on the sofa and Roby bounced over to pile on top of him. Mike looked at me and I sat down catty-corner to him, the dog sprawled between us.

"I've been thinking," Mike said. "We need to spend more time together."

When I left my apartment in Waikiki to move into Mike's house in Aiea Heights, I had given up most of the time I had spent surfing, instead hanging out with Mike, talking or going out to eat or going on long runs together. Now I couldn't remember the last run we'd taken.

I seemed to get hit with one demanding case after another that kept me at police headquarters or out on the streets of O'ahu. And Mike, a fire investigator with the Honolulu Fire Department, had been asked to review the department's procedures after a disastrous fire on the North Shore. When he wasn't at work, he was hunched over his laptop, researching other departments' policies and figuring out how to apply them to HFD.

It didn't leave either of us much time for domestic bliss, and the stress was starting to show.

"We could go on vacation together," he suggested.

I sat down on the sofa sideways, so I could face him, and Roby sprawled on the floor between us. "Yeah, we could get a cheap flight to the mainland. San Francisco? Vegas? We could get onto one of those junkets."

He crossed his arms over his chest. "I don't want to go somewhere to gamble or sightsee. I just want to hang out with you."

"And we can't do that here?"

He shook his head. "We're both tied to our beepers. Even if we took time off, something would come up and one or both of us would have to go to work."

"Then where do you want to go?" I asked.

"You ever been to Kauai?" There was something a bit too casual about the suggestion and I was immediately suspicious. Cop habits die hard.

I leaned back against the arm of the leather sofa, one of our first big joint purchases. "Long time ago. Before Iniki."

Hurricane Iniki was the deadliest hurricane to hit Hawai'i since they started keeping records. It devastated the island of Kauai. Thousands of homes had been damaged or destroyed, along with countless businesses. It had taken the island years to recover. "Why Kauai?" I asked.

"Ben Keaumoku has a timeshare there that he can't use. He's looking for someone to take it over."

Ah. That was why he'd seemed overly casual when he brought the idea up. He'd already decided what he wanted to do but wanted to pretend it was a joint decision. I got a sour feeling in my stomach.

Not that I didn't want to go to Kauai, or even that I didn't like Ben Keaumoku. Ben was one of the fire captains Mike worked with, and when Mike started taking his first tentative steps out of the closet after we got together the second time, Ben had been one of his most supportive friends.

"When?" I asked.

Mike looked down at Roby, avoiding my gaze. "Next week."

"Next week!" I squawked. "What if we can't get off work?"

He looked up. "I can. I already checked. You just have to ask."

"How long have you known about this?" I crossed my arms over my chest, too, even though I knew it was a defensive posture I shouldn't be assuming with the love of my life.

"Just today. His daughter has some kind of respiratory thing going on, and the doctor doesn't want her to travel for the next month. I checked with the chief to be sure I could get the time."

Roby sensed that his dads were getting along, and he clambered up on the sofa and snuggled between us.

I looked at my watch. It was just after seven in the evening. "When do we need to leave?"

"Can we go on Saturday? The time share is for seven days."

I picked up my cell phone. What the hell—my boss called me at home all the time.

He answered on the first ring. "Sampson."

"Hey, Lieutenant. I was wondering. Any chance I could get next week off for vacation?"

"Where do we stand with the phony valets?"

My partner, Ray Donne, and I had been working on a case for the last two weeks. Young guys in generic valet outfits had been lurking around fancy hotels and restaurants. As soon as the real valets were occupied, a phony one would jump in, hand over a fake ticket to the guest, and drive off with the car. They went straight to a chop shop that either cut them up for parts or filed off the VIN number and shipped them to Asia.

It had taken us a while to figure out the operation, and then Ray and I had swooped in and arrested four young guys, who fingered the boss of the operation. We had pulled him in that afternoon.

"With the arrest we made today, all that's left is the paperwork," I said. "I can have that done by Friday."

"Then take the week. You and Mike going somewhere?"

Lieutenant Sampson had taken a chance on me when no one else in the department would, when I had just been dragged out of the closet. Ever since then he'd been very supportive, and I appreciated the way he treated Mike as my spouse, just the way he did with Ray's wife Julie.

"Looks like we're going to Kauai," I said.

Mike called Ben to make the arrangements, and I dialed my brother Haoa and asked if Roby could come stay with him and his family while we were gone. "I don't know, brah," he said. "He might like living with us better. You come back, he won't want to leave."

"Hah. Nobody could spoil that dog the way we do." I made arrangements to drop Roby off on Saturday morning and booked an early afternoon flight and a rental car for the two of us to pick up at the airport in Lihue.

When both of us were finished with our phone calls, Mike said, "You think maybe we could get a head start on our vacation?" He tickled the inside of my thigh with his big toe.

I pushed the dog off the sofa and cuddled up next to him. Even though his body was as familiar as my own, I still loved just being next to him, our thighs and arms touching, leaning forward for a kiss. His lips met mine lightly and I turned my head a bit so we could move even closer. I reached around behind him and snaked one arm up under his T-shirt, tickling the light dusting of hair over his shoulder blades.

My dick stiffened as we kissed. He reached over and tweaked my right nipple and I groaned. He was right: we had been ignoring each other for too long. He pushed me back down onto the sofa and climbed on top of me. That was my favorite position of all, feeling his whole body pressing down on me. I even liked the way I got short of breath if he was compressing my ribcage. I think it made my orgasms better. And what the hell, he had been trained as an EMT when he was an active-duty fire-fighter, so he could always revive me if I passed out. I wondered if I'd like mouth-to-mouth resuscitation from him. Probably.

We kissed again and he began rubbing his body against mine, the friction of our clothes providing an exquisite pain as my stiff dick chafed against the cotton fabric of my boxers. Precum began to dribble out of my piss slit. I could feel my orgasm rising, and I banged my head against the pillows.

Then his cell phone rang.

I wanted to tell him to ignore it, but I knew he couldn't, just the way I couldn't ignore an emergency call from HPD.

He backed off and reached for the phone. I took a couple of deep breaths but my dick didn't go down. I could tell his didn't either.

He listened to the caller for a minute, then said, "Shit. All right, I'm on it." He hung up and extricated himself from the couch. "Suspicious fire out in Kaimuki. I've gotta go." I watched his ass as he left the room, and rubbed my dick a couple of times with my right hand. But it wasn't the same.

Mike changed from his T-shirt and shorts into his standard work outfit of khakis and an HFD polo shirt and was out of the house in minutes. I thought about pulling up some Internet porn to relieve my blue balls, but decided it was better to wait for Mike to return.

He didn't get home until I was already asleep, though, and we were so busy the next few days that we hardly spoke. Saturday morning I woke to find him standing by the side of the bed fastening his watch. He was already dressed. "Where are you going?" I asked, then yawned.

"Ben was supposed to be on call this morning but he had to take his daughter to the ER. I've got to run out to Nanakuli and check out a fire. Can you pack for me?"

Nanakuli was on the Leeward Coast, way out the Farrington Highway. If he got caught up there he'd have trouble making it to the airport for our flight. "I don't understand why you had to take it over. He knows you're going to his timeshare."

"His daughter is sick," Mike said, enunciating every word. "Have a little compassion, asshole."

"What the fuck!" I sat up in bed. "You make these plans without even asking me and then you run off?"

"I'm going to work. You don't want to go to Kauai, you can stay right here."

He stalked out of the bedroom and a moment later I heard the front door slam.

Roby clambered up into bed next to me and settled down on Mike's pillow. "That went well," I said to him.

I tried to go back to sleep but I was too antsy. Instead I got up and started to pack—for both Mike and myself. I ran out to the local Long's Drugs to pick up some travel-sized items, then went back home and got Roby, along with everything he'd need for a long weekend with his aunt and uncle and their brood of four human kids and one furry one. Sometimes I swear the dog needs more travel stuff than Mike and me: a bag of food, bowls for food and water, glucosamine and chondroitin for his joints, a selection of toys and a couple of rawhide chews, and a bag of treats shaped like little T-bone steaks.

It was noon by the time I got back to the house, and I hadn't heard from Mike. I tried his cell and the call went direct to voicemail. Was he ignoring me? Out of cell range? Had something happened at the fire?

We had a 3:00 flight on go! Airlines, and we needed to get to the airport at least an hour earlier for check-in. I started to get irritated, but stopped myself. This was going to be our vacation, and I didn't want to kick it off with more fighting. And I'm a big believer in karma: I always worried that if we argued before leaving each other, we would tempt fate to cause some accident that would make us regret our words forever.

I paced around the house for a while, then gave up and loaded the Jeep with our luggage. I tried Mike's cell again as I was driving away.

This time he picked up. "I'm just leaving the fire now. Couldn't get a signal out there. It doesn't look like I'll have a chance to get home. Can I just meet you at the airport?"

"Sure. I've got the bags. In case you're really late and I'm already at the gate, you can check in with your driver's license."

"Will do. Sorry, babe. I'll make it up to you on Kauai."

"You will. Love you."

He said he loved me, too, and hung up. I drove to the airport, parked, and lugged both our bags to the check-in desk. The airline was flying the Bombardier CJ-2000, so I had to check everything except a little daypack with our reservation information, a couple of granola bars, and a book. I walked down to the gate, resisting the urge to bug Mike by calling his cell again and asking where the fuck he was.

The gates at the Interisland Terminal are open-air, sheltered from the elements by a hipped roof, low stone walls, and hibiscus hedges. I paced around waiting for Mike as the minutes ticked by.

The plane began boarding and Mike still wasn't there. I finally broke down and dialed his cell. "We're boarding. Where are you?"

"Waiting in line for the security check. I'm almost there. Don't leave without me."

"I'll stand in front of the plane," I said dryly, and hung up.

There was a sudden gust of wind and rain began to beat down on the tarmac. The last couple of patrons scurried over to the plane's staircase and began to climb. The wind turned and the rain began to blow into the open gate area. I huddled in a corner, rubbing my upper arms against the sudden chill.

The gate was empty except for me and a couple of agents when Mike came running up. We handed over our boarding passes and hurried out over the tarmac to the plane, getting soaked in the process. We rushed up the slippery staircase and I nearly fell once as I got close to the top, but Mike was right behind me.

We made our way to our seats, dripping down the aisle, and then the flight attendant closed the door and we pushed off. "Sorry I was late," Mike said. "I really did try to get through as fast as I could."

"You talk to Ben? How's his daughter?"

"She's better. They had to put her on a respirator to help her breathe until she gets over the infection."

I realized how lucky we were to both be healthy, to have good jobs and a safe place to live and the chance to go on vacation together. I resolved not to argue the whole time we were on Kauai. If I could manage it.

The flight was brief, and while Mike dozed I looked out the window at the endless miles of ocean. We landed and walked right over to the car-rental counter. The clerk was a ditzy blonde, a recent transplant from the mainland, and she had a lot of trouble finding my reservation. "All of these names with apostrophes," she said. "It's so confusing."

"It's called an okina," I said. "Not an apostrophe."

"Enough, Kimo," Mike said. "Let Mary Sue focus on what she's doing so we can get a move on."

Her name tag actually read Louise, but I wasn't going to

correct him. She gave us directions out of the airport to Route 56, which of course were wrong and led us in a big circle. "I thought you'd been here before," Mike grumbled.

"Twenty years ago. Can't you read the map?"

Both of us were pretty ragged by the time we got to the time-share. All I wanted to do was get into a pair of shorts and a T-shirt with a very tall, very cold tropical drink in my hand. But as soon as we walked into the one-bedroom condo with a view of Poipu Beach, Mike said, "I'm going to hurl," and rushed to the bathroom.

So much for our romantic getaway, I thought. I brought all the luggage in and then went back out to get him some over-the-counter medication. He took the pills, crawled into bed, and zonked out.

I walked down the beach and stopped at the first bar I found, where they were playing Jawaiian music—a combination of Hawaiian and Jamaican reggae—and ordered a strawberry daiquiri. It was an open, thatched-roof place with a gorgeous view of the beach. The sun sparkled on wavelets that lapped at fine white sand. The shore curved around and disappeared into a lush rainforest.

I sat on a stool and drank, tapping my foot on the bar rail.

"I see you like this beat, too."

I looked to my right and saw a forty-something *haole* tourist with thinning brown hair and a bit of raccooning where he'd fallen asleep in the sun with his sunglasses on.

"Yeah, it's kind of infectious," I said.

"You mind if I join you?"

"Sure."

He sat on the barstool next to me and motioned to the bartender for a refill of his frozen margarita. "I'm Reed." He reached out to shake my hand.

"Kimo," I said. "Where are you from?" He had a good strong grip, which I liked, and he made sure to make eye contact.

"Omaha. Here for a convention of financial planners at the Hyatt. Turns out not to be as much fun as I was hoping. Everybody else brought a wife or a girlfriend."

"Let me guess. You don't have either of those."

"And haven't wanted one since I was about seventeen and figured myself out."

I nodded. "Took me a lot longer than that."

The bartender brought his daiquiri and Reed raised his glass toward me. I clinked with him and we both smiled.

My dick was swelling in my pants. Shit. What was I doing here, flirting with another guy, when I was supposed to be on a romantic weekend with Mike? But it had been a long time since another guy had expressed some interest in me. It was shady behavior and cruel to Reed, but I just wanted to savor the feeling for a few minutes. There was no real harm in flirting, anyway. I'd still end up with Mike, though if he was sick we'd probably be in separate beds.

We were the only people in the bar, and I noticed both Reed and I were tapping our feet to the beat. "You want to dance?" I asked.

"You think we can?"

"Nobody here to complain."

"Then hell, yes."

When he stood up and I got a good look at him, I could see Reed had more middle-aged spread than I'd expected, but he had some moves. He had a great sense of rhythm and he was comfortable in his body, and that came through as he danced. At first we were just doing our own thing, rocking and swaying, but then Reed took my hand and pulled me toward him and then back, and swung me around.

We danced through three songs. Out of the corner of my eye
I saw some other people start to come into the bar, but nobody
said anything. They were all on vacation, after all, and who
wants to get worked up when there's warm weather, a beautiful
view, and a well-stocked bar?

We finally quit and returned to the bar, where we ordered
another round of drinks and a pupu platter to share—some bits
of roasted pork, Chinese dumplings, and pineapple. We kept
eating and drinking and talking and laughing, and I felt a lot of
the tension in my gut begin to go away.

Then I looked up and saw Mike in the doorway of the bar.
"You left me in that condo with nothing to eat," he said.

"Well, come on over here and order something."

I didn't mean to sound irritated, but even though I knew I
wasn't going up to Reed's room with him, I was enjoying the
delicious sensation that something might happen, and Mike's
arrival harshed my mellow.

Despite his mood, Mike was still a very handsome guy, with
wavy dark hair, a black mustache with just the faintest touches
of gray, a strong jaw and a killer body. Reed's mouth hung open
as he stared at Mike. "Friend of yours?" he asked me.

"Partner." I know I sighed as I said it, and I shouldn't have.

Reed's body sagged as he realized what was going on. Then
Mike stepped into the bar and crossed over toward us, sliding
onto a stool next to Reed. He stuck his hand out. "I'm Mike."

Reed was almost too flabbergasted to respond, but he did
shake Mike's hand and introduce himself.

"They have burgers here?" Mike asked.

Reed pushed a menu toward Mike.

"You're feeling better?" I asked.

"Right as rain. Shouldn't have grabbed that chili on the way
to the airport."

I wanted to say that if he hadn't, he'd have been on time, and we wouldn't have gotten soaked on the tarmac either—but for once I kept my mouth shut.

The bartender came over, and Mike ordered a Fire Rock Pale Ale and a mushroom burger, medium well. "Sounds good to me," Reed said. "I'll have the same."

I had to be contrary, so I ordered a bacon cheeseburger, medium, and another strawberry daiquiri.

When the bartender left, Mike turned to Reed. "So where are you from?"

Reed wasn't quite sure what was going on—and neither was I. But he played along, and soon he and Mike were flirting just as he and I had been. I sat on the far side of Reed, feeling left out. This was supposed to be a sexy getaway for Mike and me—so why was Reed still between us?

I had a sexual history longer than some modern novels, first with women, then, after I came out of the closet, with a lot of different guys in different situations. By the time I met Mike, I was ready to settle down and commit to one man. He was my first real boyfriend, the first guy I fell in love with.

I was his first love, too, but he didn't have anywhere near the sexual background I had, and sometimes I thought he regretted not having sown enough wild oats. We'd see a guy covered with tats, for example, and Mike would wonder what sex with him would be like. Or we'd be watching a porn movie and see a guy with a Prince Albert, with pierced nipples or bars through the frenum, the scrotum, or the perineum, and he'd wonder what that would be like.

He'd never been with a black man or a guy in his senior years, though he'd had some interesting experiences with a leather daddy in Waikele that he remembered fondly.

The bartender delivered our burgers and Mike bit into his

lustily. "This is great," he said. Then he turned to Reed. "So, you into threesomes?"

I nearly choked on my burger. Mike knew damn well that I didn't want to share him; he was all mine. He'd expressed interest in threesomes in the past, but only in the most general sense—and I'd shut him down every time.

Reed was quicker on the uptake than I was. I figure he guessed Mike's interest as soon as he sat down at the bar with us. He looked Mike in the eye and said, "Having sex with a stud as handsome as you is a wet dream for a guy like me. The two of you, as gorgeous and built as you are? I'd feel like I died and went to heaven."

"Well, don't die on us just yet." He licked his lips. "What about you, K-man?"

Mike has a million nicknames for me: K-man, Keeper, King Kong Kimo. When he uses one of them I know he's teasing. But who was he teasing—Reed? Or Me?

My dick had already made its vote. I was hard the whole time I danced with Reed, and I was sure he'd noticed the tiny wet spot on my jeans. I shriveled up as soon as Mike walked in, like an embarrassed kid caught with his hand in the candy jar. But once Mike mentioned a threesome, my dick pronged up again.

I took a deep breath. I knew couples who had broken up, and one of the first signs their relationship had shown of going south was when they opened up to other people. But I also knew a couple in Kahala who had been merrily engaging in all kinds of sex, either together, separately, or with one or more others, and they were just as much in love as they'd ever been.

Reed put his hand on my thigh. "What do you say?"

My skin tingled from his touch. I drained the last of my drink and said, "Whose place is closer?"

"My hotel's right next door, and I've got a king-sized bed," Reed said.

"Sounds like a winner," Mike said.

We dropped some cash on the bar and Reed led the way out. Mike reached for my shoulder. "This is all right with you, isn't it?"

Was I going to be honest and say no? That all I wanted was to go back to the time share together and fuck our brains out, just the two of us? The look in his eyes said this was something he wanted, and it wasn't like he was asking me to do something painful or degrading. "I love you. If you want to do this then I'm right there with you."

He leaned over and kissed me. "That's my K-Man."

We went in a side door of the hotel and Reed led us to his room, which had a lanai overlooking the beach. As soon as the door was closed, Mike said, "Here's the deal, Reed. Kimo is too bossy sometimes, and he won't do what I tell him to. How about you? You do what you're told?"

"Yes, sir," Reed said. I could see his dick was rock hard and pressing against his cargo shorts.

"Good," Mike said. "Here's what I want you to do first. Get naked."

It was almost comical to watch Reed hurry to unbutton and toss off his aloha shirt, then drop his shorts to the group and step out of them. He was wearing a pair of generic white briefs, and as he pulled them down his stiff dick bounced out.

"Well, now, that's a nice surprise," Mike said, as he and I both noticed the barbell at the base of Reed's dick. I guess Omaha is a more exciting place than I thought.

"I know, I need to work out more," Reed said, pinching the flesh at his waist.

"You look just fine to me," Mike said. "Now I want you to

take off Kimo's shirt."

I shivered at Reed's touch as he began undoing the buttons of my shirt. Without prompting he leaned down and took my right nipple between his teeth as he finished shucking my shirt. I moaned with pleasure.

It was weird to feel this man working on my nipples—and the sexual pull that resulted—and yet look up and see Mike watching, not participating. He was the only man I'd been with since we reunited, and it was strange and yet very sexy to be with someone else—especially with Mike right there.

Mike stepped up close to me and I wondered if he was going to push Reed away. Instead Mike kissed me as Reed continued to work, using his fingers on the nipple he wasn't sucking. It was almost too much sexual input—I felt overwhelmed.

Mike was still fully clothed. He reached down and unbuckled my belt, then pushed my shorts and boxers down. I shimmied out of them and kicked off my deck shoes, so that I was as naked as Reed.

Reed reached down and palmed my dick, and the feel of his hand, soft and a bit sweaty, was so different from what I was accustomed to—Mike's work-hardened hands, the way he wrapped his hand around my dick and teased the head with his thumb.

"That's it," Mike said, stepping back. "Work his dick. Get him all juiced up."

Reed continued his nipple play and began rubbing the flat of his hand up and down over my dick. As I watched, Mike pulled his polo shirt up over his head. He'd been working out more, and his abs rippled as he reached up and pulled it off, then tossed it to the dresser across from the king-sized bed.

I felt a pang of love and longing as Mike unbuttoned his jeans, then unzipped them. He wore a pair of white cotton low-riding briefs, a stark contrast to his tanned chest and the silky black hair that covered most of his body. He stepped out of his running shoes and kicked off his jeans. His dick was stiff and already leaking precum onto his shorts, but he kept them on.

Reed wrapped his hand around my dick, slippery with precum, and began to work it up and down. Mike stood there and watched for a minute, then asked, "So tell me, Reed. What's your pleasure? You like to suck or get sucked? Fuck or get fucked?"

Reed looked up at him, glassy-eyed with lust. "Whatever you like."

Mike nodded. "Well, then, down on your knees, pal, and open your mouth."

Reed obeyed, and took most of my dick down his throat. The feeling of warmth and wet was so overwhelming I almost came right there.

Mike pulled down his shorts and stepped out of them, leaving them on the hotel room carpet, but I wasn't about to complain. He leaned close to me once again and began kissing me. I felt his hand stroking my lower back, and he half turned so that his dick was close to Reed's mouth.

Without any prompting Reed switched from me to Mike. My dick was so hard it ached, and the drying saliva on it was cold in the air-conditioned air. "That's it," Mike said. "Get my dick nice and wet so it'll slide right into the K-Man."

Reed pulled off for a second and said, "I have rubbers in my bag."

"Nobody goes into the K-man's ass except me, so we won't be needing them right now," Mike said. "But thanks for the offer."

He gently pulled out of Reed's mouth and stepped behind me. As Reed resumed sucking me, Mike grabbed my shoulders and positioned himself at my ass. Then, with one hand prying open my ass, he slammed his dick into me, his pubic hair scratching against my globes.

If I hadn't been so swamped by lust it would have hurt like a bastard. But instead the pain was absorbed into the endorphins surging through my blood stream and all I did was moan and lick my lips.

Then Mike gripped my hips and started banging me, fast and furious. Tears welled up at the corners of my eyes. I felt like my ass was being plunged by a power drill. A soaring pleasure shook me all the way down to my toes.

"I'm gonna…" I began, and Reed clamped his lips down on my dick and suctioned for all he was worth, and I squinted my eyes shut to focus on my pleasure. The orgasm surged through me and I saw stars behind my eyelids. My arms and legs were like jelly and I felt myself standing only because Mike was holding me up. The cum rose from my balls and spurted out into Reed's mouth as my body shook with the power of my orgasm.

I clenched my ass tight to hold onto the sensation and Mike groaned behind me, slamming one last time into me and leaning his head back and howling. I felt the hot rocket of his cum coating my ass chute, and I flexed my muscles on him in the way I knew he liked. He stayed in me as his dick softened.

Reed backed off and sat back against the bed as Mike and I disengaged. Reed's dick was still hard. "That was frigging awesome," he said.

"And you didn't even cum," I said. "Stand up."

He did, grabbing onto the bed for a hand up. I went down to the carpet and wrapped my lips around the head of his dick, which was already loose with precum. Mike stuck his right index finger in Reed's mouth and said, "Suck my finger, Reedie, so I can use it to fuck you."

Reed's eyes opened even wider, and he took Mike's finger into his mouth. A moment later Mike pulled it out and reached around behind Reed. I could tell when the finger penetrated him because his dick jumped in my mouth. He didn't last more than a minute longer, and then he was shooting off such a load in my mouth that the cum was dripping out one side no matter how hard I tried to contain it.

I stood up shakily, and saw that Mike was kissing Reed. I wanted some of that action so I pushed my face in there, a confusion of tongues and lips and chins. Then Mike wrapped one arm around me and one around Reed, and he fell back to the bed, taking us with him.

It took us a minute to get ourselves organized—Mike flat on his back in the center, me on my side facing him, Reed facing him from the other side. Mike extended his arms so that one was behind Reed's shoulders and one behind mine, and the three of us dozed off, surrounded by the tang of sweat and sex and the afterglow of an amazing exertion.

Mike woke first. I felt him stirring beside me as he extricated his arm from beneath Reed, who was snoring gently. Mike pushed at me, and I got up off the bed. "Get your stuff and let's go," he said.

"What about…"

"He's sleeping with the angels. And when he wakes up he'll have some amazing memories," Mike whispered.

We dressed quickly and as quietly as we could, while Reed continued to sleep, and then we slipped out the door of his hotel room, both of us carrying our shoes in our hands. The tails of Mike's polo shirt were outside his pants, and my shirt was buttoned funny. Mike looked at me and started to laugh, and I joined him.

All the tension I'd been feeling for past few weeks was gone.

I remembered that Mike wasn't only my lover and life partner, he was my best friend. And instead of driving us further apart, bringing another guy into the bedroom with us had brought us back together.

"You okay?" he asked, as we started down the beachfront path back toward the condo.

"Better than okay. How about you?"

"I'm great. You're not freaked out?"

I shook my head. "I don't think the solution to our problems is going to be bringing a parade of different guys through our bedroom—but I have to admit that scene was very hot."

I realized something else. No one was ever going to know me as well as Mike did, and vice versa. Sex was only one part of our relationship. Our connection went way beyond that, down to almost a cellular level. I realized that I wasn't so scared of sharing him anymore.

"As long as we're barefoot, what if we walk back along the beach?" I asked. "We can pretend we're just a pair of beach bums and all we've got to do for the next couple of days is eat, sleep, and make love."

"Pretend, hell," Mike said. "That's exactly what we're going to do."

HOT FUN IN THE SUMMERTIME

Shane Allison

I grab my tray from the What-A-Burger clerk and start to turn around when I feel a tap on my right shoulder. I hate when people do that. I turn around and there he is.

"Hey, Cray, what's going on?"

This brotha stands before me. He is slightly taller than me, with hair cut close to his scalp, wearing a polo shirt, jeans, and brown deck shoes.

"Hey, how you doin'." Of course I have no damn clue who he is, but I say hey anyway just to be nice.

"You don't remember me, do you? It's me, Delroy, from Rickards High." It's still not enough to jog my memory, but I play the shit off like I know who he is. I don't want to be rude.

"Oh, hey, man!"

I walk to my booth with my food. As I sit there, I can't help but stare, admiring Delroy from the back corner of the restaurant. I keep trying to place his face. I would have remembered someone as fine as him. I keep looking as I unfurl my chicken sandwich out of the flimsy orange wax paper. I'm impressed by his bubble booty in his jeans as I squeeze spicy ketchup on my shoestring French fries. Maybe he thinks I'm someone else? I don't know, but damn, he's cute. Delroy slaps me out of my gaze when he turns and looks back. Our eyes meet for a second before I stare down at my fries drowning in ketchup. As I bite into my sandwich, Delroy starts toward me. *Damn. What does he want now?*

Delroy towers over me like a giant, like he's a man on a mission.

"You don't remember me, do you?" Delroy asks.

With my mouth stuffed with food, I hope he will let me finish chewing before I can answer his question. I swallow hard.

"I'm sorry, man, not a clue. I thought you were this guy from Movies 8 I used to work with back in the nineties."

"Naw, it's cool. You mind if I join you?" My heart skips a beat. I'm a little annoyed, but I figure since we're old classmates...

"Yeah, sure," I say. Delroy starts to take his food out of his bag.

"I don't see too many people around here anymore from Rickards."

"Well, it's Tallahassee. I understand why no one would want to stick around. I think if I saw someone from high school, I would probably walk the other way." Much like what I want to do with Delroy.

"Why you say that?" Delroy asks as he stuffs a couple of fries into his mouth.

"I left all of that behind me as soon as I walked off the stage with my diploma. The best thing about leaving high school is that you get a chance to totally reinvent yourself—and I was in dire need of a makeover."

Delroy chuckles when I say that. "Those were probably the worst years of my young loser life. So what are you doing now?"

I think of something that will sound impressive. "Studying broadcast journalism. So what about you? What have you been up to?"

"I'm running my own lumber mill business down in St. Marks. I got about fifty guys working for me down there."

Delroy has big, deep, puppy-dog-brown eyes. Judging from the nicks and healed cuts on his hands, he is no stranger to hard work. That or he stuck his hand in a meat grinder.

"That's impressive, wow."

"I do all right. It's a living. Hey, do you remember Mr. Henderson?" he asks, randomly changing the subject. "He taught tenth-grade science."

"You mean Papa Smurf?" I say.

Delroy starts to grin. "Yeah, everybody called him that 'cause of his beard. Remember that field trip to Apalachicola he took all of us on? You wouldn't get in the water and just sat there on the beach with your clothes on."

It isn't until he mentions that field trip that it all starts to come back to me.

"Shit, now I remember you, man."

"You do?" Delroy says.

"You were wearing like these orange trunks that day."

"I used to always try and pick you up and throw you over my shoulder, you remember that?"

"Yeah you were pretty strong for your age back then."

I recall the way the beach water trickled off his chest, over the hills of abs and pecs. Fuck, he was beautiful.

"Everybody was laughing because I was yelling, asking you to put me down."

"Yep. That shit was funny."

It was funny for you and everybody else, yeah, I think, mustering up a halfhearted grin. It just reminds me how much I hated Rickards. "I don't remember seeing you after tenth grade. Whatever happened to you?"

"My mama moved us out of that zone. I ended up going to Wakulla High. I always thought you were a cool guy," Delroy says before taking a sip from his cup. "I remember that poem you wrote in Mrs. Forbes's class."

"Oh shit, you remember that? That was so stupid. She made me read it in front of the whole class."

"It's in my yearbook in some old boxes back at my beach house."

"No fuckin' way! You kept that shit?"

"I don't know. I liked it. I guess seeing you made me think about the poem."

"Well, I'm glad *somebody* liked it."

Delroy and I finish eating our fast-food meal. "You should come out to the beach house sometime. Hang out, have a beer."

The excitement that I feel when he invites me out to his beach house is like hot sparks going off in me, so of course I accept. "It's been years since I've been out to St. Marks."

"Good. It'll be cool to have some company. I'll put on a couple of steaks, a few baked potatoes. What kind of beer you like?"

"Any kind is fine as long as it's not Guinness."

"How 'bout Blue Moon?"

"I didn't know you could read minds. I love Blue Moon."

"Oh, I'm a master of many trades," Delroy grins. "How bout Friday night? I saw on the news this morning that it's supposed to be a full moon—and a full moon looks great from the beach, man."

I don't want to think it, but it sounds like a date. Delroy and I walk outside to his red muscle Hemi truck parked next to my Buick that's a piece of shit, but gets me from A to B.

"I wrote my cell down just in case you get lost."

"I shouldn't have a problem finding you."

I don't admit to Delroy that I'm terrible with directions. His thumb grazes mine as he hands me his number. "So Friday around eight-ish?"

"I'll be there." Our hands come together in a handshake. "It was good seeing you again, man."

"Same here. Get home safe," I tell him.

Those four days come and go. I think about Delroy 24/7, about how good it was seeing him after all these years. I feel bad about lying to him, telling him I'm still in school. It bugs me enough that I decide I'm going to come clean, tell him at dinner what's really up. Friday comes. I'm a mess of nerves. I can barely function at work. On my way home, I stop by the liquor store to get a bottle of wine. I just don't feel right showing up and not bringing anything.

Judging from the directions he gave, I'm on the right road. I start to see the names of the signs he wrote down. My car radio clock reads 8:16 p.m. I turn left onto a narrow gravel road. The light coming from the full moon lights my way. Delroy was right. It's a beautiful beach. I drive until I see a white two-story beach house. It's just like he described. I know I'm in the right place when I spot his truck in the driveway. I ease up next to the stallion of red and steel. I grab the bottle of wine off the seat and start for the front door. I can see smoke coming from the roof of the beach house. The faint smell of charred meat mixes with the cool beach air. I'm so excited, maybe too excited. I ring the doorbell.

"Cray, up here," I hear Delroy holler. I walk around to the side of the house where Delroy is looking down from his deck at me. The background of the moon looks amazing behind him. "Hey, come on up."

I push open the picket gate into Delroy's beach backyard. The breeze coolly kisses my cheek.

"This place is gorgeous."

"Ain't it, though? I love it out here."

"And this house. This is... wow, I mean—"

"Thank you." Delroy's smile puts the gleam from the moon to shame.

"Would you like a tour of the place after dinner?"

"Yeah, sure."

"What's this?" He looks at the bottle in my hand.

"I didn't feel right coming empty-handed. It's not much. Hope you like white wine."

"I do, thank you." Delroy takes the libation and sets the bottle in the chest of ice with the beer. "We'll have it with our steaks. Speaking of which, how do you like yours?"

"Well done," I say.

"I prefer my cow with a little pink inside, so that's where we differ," Delroy laughs, as he turns the steaks on the grill.

"I've never had it like that before. I'm just so used to eating my steak cooked clean through."

"You should try medium rare. It's really good."

"Medium rare it is, then." I smile.

"Good boy," says Delroy. The table is decorated with blue-and-yellow place mats. "Would you mind keeping an eye on the steaks while I go get the salad?"

"Yeah, sure." I take a whiff of my shirt. *Damn. I put too much cologne on.*

I look out onto the beach; the thick, white gleam from the moon is gorgeous against the water. "I can't believe I'm really here," I say.

"Believe it," Delroy says, returning with a bowl of salad and salt and pepper shakers. I didn't realize he heard me.

"So this is what you wake up to every morning?"

"You should see it during the day. This might sound like the worst cliché, but I don't care. I love taking long walks out here to clear my head, breathe a little."

"I can see why you love it out here."

Delroy places the salad and shakers on the table, then lifts the lid off the grill. A fat blanket of smoke evaporates into the cool June air.

"Looks like these are done. We can eat." Delroy forks the two steaks onto a serving platter and sets them on the dinner table next to the salad.

I sit down and spoon modest portions of the greenery onto both of our plates alongside our steaks as Delroy screws the cork off the wine and pours. This spread beats a TV dinner any day of the week. Delroy sits across from me. Our knees kiss under the table. He raises his glass to make a toast.

"To old friends," Delroy says.

"To old friends." We take sips from the wine I brought. It's good, with a slight sweet aftertaste. "I have a confession to make."

"Wassup?" Delroy says.

"I wasn't completely truthful with you last week. I'm not in school anymore."

"Okay," Delroy says, poking at his salad with his fork.

"I work part-time at a movie theater. I've been there for three years and I hate every inch, crack, and crevice of that place."

Delroy let loose a loud guffaw, which isn't what I expected.

"What?"

"Man, that ain't nothing to be ashamed of. At least you have a job, right?"

"I finished grad school in New York back in 2003."

Delroy looks at me smiling with those happy, puppy-brown eyes. "In journalism?" Delroy asks.

"An MFA in English. Creative writing."

"Whyjoo lie?" Delroy asks.

"'Cause I didn't want you to think that I was a loser. My folks are always telling me, 'All that education and you work at a movie theater?' So I just make something up that sounds a lot better than saying I work at a movie theater."

"You shouldn't be ashamed of what you do and you sure as hell shouldn't be ashamed of what you have accomplished. I kind of knew about the grad school stuff and you being published."

"How?" I ask, as I cut into my steak.

"I Googled you. I didn't think anything would come up, but I was surprised to find all this stuff on you. The books. The poems. I spent like most of the day reading your poems. You definitely have the goods, man. I'm proud of you."

Did he just say that he was proud of me?

Delroy has said something to me that no one in my family has ever said. I feel myself getting teary-eyed, but I hold back. I'm not about to break down like a punk in front of him. I start to feel a little embarrassed knowing that Delroy has read my work, especially the more erotic stuff.

"So how's your steak?" Delroy asks.

"I love the spice I'm getting. It's delicious."

"Cool. I'm glad you like it," Delroy says as he pulls a piece of the steak into his mouth from the tip of the fork.

"If I lived out here, I would never leave. I bet it's a great place to come out and write." I say.

"Well, I'm glad that you could come out. Other than my son, I don't do a whole lot of entertaining. It's beautiful, yeah, but it gets lonely sometimes."

"So what happened to you after high school?"

"I worked at my dad's lumber business. Leandra was a receptionist there when I met her. We started to date, got married, and had Kendrick a year later. It was nice for a while, but I started to see this fucked-up side to her after Kendrick was born. I wanted it to work, but the more we tried, the more I felt myself slipping away. Leandra wanted more than what I could give."

"It's her loss, losing a good man like you. You have your health, you own your own successful business, you have a son you're proud of."

"Yeah, I'm blessed. That boy means the world to me," says Delroy. "Well, on that note, why don't we have the rest of our wine on the beach?"

We make our way out onto the white, sandy shore. "Take your shoes off. The sand feels great between your toes." I kick off my shoes. The beach feels cool under my feet as we stroll. I want to reach out and take his hand, but I'm too scared he's going to freak out.

"Let's go for a swim."

"I don't have any trunks."

"Hell, who needs swim trunks?"

I watch as Delroy starts to unbutton his shirt. *Holy shit*, I thought. "Naked?" I yell.

"Why not? We the only ones out here."

His sinewy, apple butter-brown physique is beautiful against the backdrop of the night. He starts to undo his jeans.

"Shit, you're serious."

Delroy just grins, stepping out of his pants. He's not wearing any underwear. Before I know anything, I'm looking at two firm ass cheeks, much more chocolaty than the rest of him. Delroy runs toward the water until it comes to his mid-thigh.

"Come on. It feels good."

"Fuck it," I say to myself, and start to strip. Before long I'm booty-naked, dick hanging soft in the open air. I rush toward the water to join Delroy. "AHHH, SHIT! COLD! COOOLD! COLD, COLD, COOOOLD!!!" I holler out as soon as the water hits my skin. Delroy starts splashing me. I fight back, shoveling water into his face.

"See, it's not so bad. I don't know what you were so afraid of all those years ago on the field trip."

The two of us stand waist-deep. "You know, the only thing I remember about that day was you."

"Whatchu mean?" Delroy smiles.

"The way you came up out of the water. It was like you were the only guy there, like everybody else had disappeared. That sounds sappy, I know."

"Not at all. No one has ever said stuff like that about me."

"Sorry. It's weird."

"No, not at all. I'm flattered, really, thank you."

Delroy and I are standing close, facing each other. My heart pounds like the water against our bodies. I feel shy about what I just said and want to take the words back and lock them away in me somewhere.

"I'm freezing," I say.

"Me too. Let's go back to the beach house. I have some towels upstairs for us to dry off with." We grab our clothes and head back. I glance for like two seconds at his dick. Delroy's balls are big and hang low. Unlike me, the cold water has no effect on his well-hung appendage. I'm glad I'm not hard. Talk about embarrassing. I follow Delroy inside. The house is sultry apart from the frigid beach breeze. His back faces me. I bask in his nakedness as he pulls two towels from a bathroom towel rack.

"That felt good. I needed that," Delroy says as he dabs at his torso with the towel. I start to get hard every time my eyes wander to his dick. *Not now*, I think. *Go down. Please go down.* But there is nothing I can do but stand there hard.

"I'm going to take a shower," he says.

"That's cool. I'll just—finish getting dressed out here."

"You can if you want."

"Ummm...."

"I mean you can wait after I'm done. It's up to you. I just thought, why waste the water?" *This on our first date? I hope he doesn't think I'm easy.* Delroy reaches past the plastic shower curtain and turns the knobs. The bathroom quickly starts to fill with steam. Delroy steps in and with my eyes glued to his booty, I follow. The shower is big enough for both of us.

He grabs the bar of deodorant soap from the shower caddy and soaps up his chest before he hands the bar to me. Delroy runs his hands along his stomach and arms, down his legs and thighs. Soapy water trickles from our bodies, off the tips of our dicks. This is really happening. It's anything but a dream. My dick is bone-hard. I start to run my hands along his chest.

"Turn around. I'll get your back," I say. I caress soft, round shoulders, knead muscle all the way to the trench of Delroy's ass. I slide between his arms, around his stomach, run my fingers up across his nips. He arches his head back. Our lips touch. My dick traces his ass. I take Delroy's dick in my hand, giving steady jerks, squeezing the head. Delroy switches the water off. "I think we're clean enough," he says.

Water streams down our naked brown bodies. We start to dry each other off. My dick aches. I drop to my knees on the vanilla bathroom rug. I take him into my mouth. I can taste the soap on his dick.

"Damn, that feels good."

Delroy sucks his teeth as I take his dick down my throat. He presses his hand at the back of my head.

This goes on for minutes until I stop. I don't want Delroy to come yet. We are dry. We move to his bedroom, which is huge and roomy with a sky-high ceiling. He tosses back the covers. I can't stop looking at his dick. I want Delroy inside me. His lips feel like clouds against mine. Our bodies kiss; our dicks graze. I start sucking his nips like hard chocolate; my tongue tickles one and then the other.

We collapse onto his bed. Delroy's skin is soft from the soap. Our bodies are warm. I can feel his dick against my inner thigh, our wine-stained tongues in each other's mouths.

"I've wanted to do this all night. I just didn't want you to think I was too forward," he says.

"Me too."

"Hold on," he says. Delroy gets up and walks over to one of the bedside tables. I know where this is going. Delroy plucks out a column of gold packets and a bottle of lube. I hang playfully off the side of his bed.

"Looks like you're still hungry," he says. Armed with the rubbers and oil, Delroy straddles me. He runs his dick along the ball of my chin, the curves of my lips, leaving traces of his juices. I ease my mouth open. I wrap my lips tight around it as I grab hold of his ass. Delroy's body is electric. I think to slide a finger in. Delroy eases away.

"You want to do the honors?" Delroy asks, handing me one of the rubbers.

I tear open the cellophane wrapping with my teeth. Greasy latex. I'm about to roll it on his dick when he says, "Can you put it on with your mouth?"

That's so kinky. I place the thick ring of the prophylactic between my lips. Delroy aims his dick up to my mouth as I start to push the latex down his shaft. I keep on until I feel his pubes tickle my nose. I slide off his dick. I position myself on my elbows and knees, and my back arches about as much as a guy my size can manage. I'm nervous, yeah, about getting fucked, but excited to feel him inside me.

"It might be better if you lie on your stomach 'cause you're so tall." I start to feel the strain with all the weight. I gotta get my big ass to a gym.

"Okay," I say.

"I just want you to be comfortable."

"Either way is cool with me," I lie.

"This is going to feel cold going in." I start to feel like a patient in some examining room. I'm ready for whatever. I hear Delroy flip open the top of the bottle and then a slight bite of cool when the lube makes contact with my ass, trickling along the walls of my crack and asshole like liquid candy. The grease feels so slippery in my booty. My dick throbs. I feel Delroy's finger suddenly. I start to tense up.

"I'll be gentle," Delroy says. I believe him. He slides his finger in deeper.

"You're pretty tight."

"It's been a while." I ball his sheets in my fists.

"You feel that?"

"Yeah, it feels goooood."

"I'm all the way up to my knuckle."

"Damn, really?"

"Yeah," Delroy grins. I arch my ass back a bit as he works my hole.

"Don't stop," I plead.

"Yeah, it sounds and *feels* like you ready."

I feel like I'm about to burst, I'm so fucking horny. I ease onto my belly. I can feel Delroy's weight on me. I feel the blunt knob of his dick head slip between my gape. He pushes. I take short, tempered breaths. It slips in like a thief. I unclench the sheets. Delroy starts to fuck me slow.

"Damn. Yeah, that's good." Delroy's kisses are red-hot along my neck, my spine. With every thrust, Delroy slides in deeper. He slides his arms under mine, pinning me down with muscled brawn. I have no choice but to take the deep dicking he's giving me. This man can fuck.

I can feel Delroy's thatch against my booty. His thrusts quicken and he grunts like a bull on top of me.

Damn, is this happening? If this is a dream, I don't want to wake up.

"Are you okay? I'm not hurting you, am I?"

"That feels nice."

Delroy's fuck-work quickens with each thrust. I moan through our kissing. Our southern hearts pound in my ears. My toes flex.

"Stay with me tonight," he whispers, his hot words in my ear.

"Yes."

Delroy reaches over my big hips for my dick, his fingers still greasy from the lube. I didn't know how hungry I was for a good fuck until now. Our bodies are sticky with sweat. I can feel my dick hard under my belly. Our fingers intertwine as Delroy sucks my earlobes.

"Shit yeah," says Delroy. He's ready to come. He keeps at me, his fingers pressing forcefully between the grooves of mine, as he holds me hostage with dick up my ass. "Mmm... Such a sweet ass," he goes on.

"Give it to me!" I say. Suddenly, I can feel him filling me, jets of juices in the rubber, up my ass. Delroy starts to ease out of me. Cool air sweeps across our bodies.

"That was great," I say. I think he's done with me now, that he got what he wanted. Delroy falls into me, back into bed. He presses his lips to mine.

"You serious about me staying the night?" I ask.

He wraps his arms around me. "Of course." We make love twice that night, until we're exhausted. Delroy looks like an angel when he sleeps. I cuddle up to him, snake my arm around his taut torso. His skin feels like warm syrup. I doze off, joining him in sleep.

FOUR-MAN
BEACH
VOLLEYBALL

Gregory L. Norris

B alls, big and white, a dozen, a *hundred*, spilled out of the sky.

Jonny Hutching met them as they sailed into range, pumping his fists, knuckling the volleyballs over the net before a single one reached the sand. In response to the pressure, his own balls threatened to shrivel out of their usual loose state. Cold sweat tickled him unpleasantly along his spine, armpits, and behind his sac. *Balls*, a thousand, rained down from a cloudless dream-sky the color of comfortable denim. He would miss some; one man, alone against the deluge—it was inevitable.

A voice in Hutch's thoughts told him that he was no longer the big man on the beach, that for five of the last ten years he'd worked in a lumberyard for shit wages, talked about behind his back by coworkers and customers alike. That voice took on Cameron Ford's inflections.

"Fucking loser," it taunted.

Hutch told it to shut the fuck up, but his mouth refused to

cooperate. More balls rained down, their shadows in the day's blinding glare adding to the confusion, making Hutch's heart gallop and his nuts shrink. Alone—

Right before Hutch jolted awake in the darkness, his eyes wide, his flesh soaked in sweat, he caught sight of another body, male, moving among the downpour of volleyballs. It wasn't Cameron. He wasn't alone, not anymore.

A shout clawed its way up his throat. At the last instant, recognition dawned and Hutch clamped his teeth together, trapping the sound before it could emerge. A layer of invisible ice formed over his perspiration, conjuring a chill. He fought the shiver, failed. As it tumbled, the gallop of his pulse slowed and the reassuring crash of the Pacific Ocean beyond the bedroom's open windows reached his ears. He choked down a dry swallow, licked his lips, tasted ass.

"You okay, dude?" asked the younger man on the other side of the bed, confirming what the dream—the nightmare—had attempted to show him, right before shorting out.

Hutch exhaled before answering, expelling the bottled breath that contained the silenced shout. "Yeah," he lied.

Then he pulled back the covers and slipped out of bed.

Long minutes later, Rio joined him in the darkness of the unlit patio. "Nerves?"

"Something like that. Ghosts."

On his way out of the beach shack, Hutch had somehow managed to pull on his boxer-briefs; the same pair, dark gray, he'd worn leading up to the previous night's sweaty bedroom games. Rio had skipped that part and sat naked on the bench beside him, his uncut dick up again, flouncing between spread legs. The urge to reach out and grope it tempted Hutch: to roll his thumb in firm, short circles across its throat while tickling the meaty nuts beneath. In short time that summer, each man had learned where the other got off on being touched.

A hypnotic soundtrack of waves crashing onto beach drifted in the background. Rio set a hand on Hutch's right knee and caressed the length of hairy leg above it: one of those places Hutch liked to be touched. Loved.

"I used to watch you on TV," Rio said, his voice melting the last of the dream's ice. His caresses woke other parts from slumber.

"I know," said Hutch, his mouth still dry.

"Every summer, dude. I always cheered for you. You made me love beach volleyball."

Hutch exhaled. "You already told me."

"What I didn't tell you was how *hard* it made me, watching you. I grew up near the beach. Used to love to gaze at hot dudes on Los Hombres. Sometimes, they'd spread their legs, go to scratch their balls, and a nut or the head of their dicks would fall out by mistake. I kept hoping you'd slip up and show us your junk when the camera cut to you."

Hutch chuckled. "For real?"

Rio nodded, his outline a degree darker than the surrounding night. "Fuck yeah. Man, you on the sand court was *poetry*. Those legs and feet..."

"You want to see my junk?" Hutch growled, mischief in his voice.

Rio's hand moved higher and yanked aside Hutch's underwear. Both balls tumbled out to dangle in the sultry darkness. Another deft move and Hutch's cock joined Rio's in the open. A warm breeze kissed his maleness one step ahead of his eager pupil, who lowered himself between Hutch's knees. The younger man's lips greeted his cock. Fingers teased his nuts with gentle tugs. Rio opened wider. The tugs that followed were less gentle.

"*Fuck*," Hutch said.

He leaned back and savored the attention and, for a short while, all of his worries evaporated, driven out by happy groans.

A moment of disbelief washed over Hutch, paralyzing him on the spot. Even his eyes, hidden behind shades, forgot to blink. His lungs emptied. Only his mind could move about and flex its limbs, meandering back to the last time he stood on this stretch of Los Hombres Beach, under the same circumstance. The footprints from his bare size twelves had likely intersected the ones he had made a decade ago, during his twenties.

The trip to the past was brief; Hutch's palsy shattered and his heart restarted, jolted back to life by the friendly smack of a hand against his butt.

"Come on, dude," said Rio, moving past.

Hutch blinked. A drop of sweat stung his left eye, his squint hidden behind his sunglasses. He remembered to inhale and drew in a breath rich with the smell of salt air, coconut sunscreen, and a hint of fresh sweat, male and clean—Rio's.

Nodding, Hutch stole a glance at the other man's lenses. The twin mirrors sent back his reflection: neat, dark hair going silver above the ears, the crow's feet around his sapphire eyes, a gruffness in his expression from the last ten years. The day-old scruff on his cheeks, chin, and throat lent his image a don't-fuck-with-me vibe, clear even to him.

"Let's do this," Hutch growled and resumed walking.

They marched across Los Hombres in the direction of the beach volleyball sand court, impossible to miss with its bleachers and banners, camera zip lines and announcer's booth. The latest sponsors were a bottled-water giant and one of the Big Five carmakers bailed out by the government in '09. Trickle-down, thought Hutch; they could afford to pay things forward, to bail him and the new league out of the mess that had befallen the old.

His emotions, equal parts confidence and worry, built with his steps. Hutch wondered if all soldiers experienced the same mix of bravado and anxiety when they set booted feet on foreign sand. Los Hombres was familiar, home soil, and his feet were bare, not booted, his soles tingling with electric pinpricks as they absorbed light and energy from the sun-warmed grains. But in the final leg, it could have been Kabul or Mogadishu or the desert wastelands leading into Baghdad. Not real warfare, he knew, nothing near the level of sacrifice American soldiers were asked to make. Still, a battle would soon brew, resulting in sweat instead of bloodshed.

The other soldier in his unit of two men faced him through sunglasses. A smile challenged Hutch's game face at the image around those eyes: six solid feet of lean muscle, smooth above the ring of fur surrounding his belly button, plenty of hair beneath. A great set of legs. Flip-flops showcased feet that were equally magnificent. His dark blue jam shorts matched the pair hanging off Hutch's hips. A dimple on one cheek greeted Hutch when his eyes returned up to Rio's.

They tapped knuckles. Hutch licked his mouth and noted Rio's phantom taste through the dregs of toothpaste, one of the two choicest pieces of ass Hutch had ever eaten. Then, together, the two men entered the sand court, where the second of those two best assholes upon which Hutch's tongue knew the honor of feasting waited.

Cameron Ford stood on the other side of the net, arms folded.

His former teammate and ally. Now, the enemy.

* * *

"So here's how it's gonna go down," Cameron said and spread his legs.

The beach towel opened, its flaps unfolding on either side of the man's muscled thighs. Cameron's cock, already stiff, jumped out of cover and pulsed upright under its own power. The two shaved balls hanging beneath spilled along the inside of his leg. Cameron gave them a tug before pumping on his cock, conjuring a cloudy tear from his pee-hole.

Troy Kearns crossed his arms, coughed to clear his throat. "Let me guess—I want to be your new partner out there on Los Hombres, I gotta prove you and me are a good fit, right?"

Cameron's smirk widened, exposing a length of clean white teeth. "You're smarter than I gave you credit for."

"Smarter than I look?" Troy challenged.

Cameron absorbed the full image of the young man before him—a former college volleyball stud who'd gone on to win gold in the Olympics. Fucker had more than that bit of pedigree going for him now that classes were out of session; bragging rights to the medal hanging in his bedroom were still good for free drinks at the local sports bar, but little else. Kearns, with his short, sandy hair and scruffy goatee, reminded him of Hutch for all the right reasons and few of the wrong, at least at this point in the negotiations. Dude had balls, for a start. After their initial workout, he'd made sure to look when they were soaping up. Big ones, as he'd suspected—loose and full of juice, dangling beneath a decent dick.

Cameron squeezed his by the root and grinned. "You're looking smarter by the second."

"Thanks."

"Don't thank me yet. You still haven't proven anything. I'm not convinced."

Troy drew in a deep breath. Dude knew the score, Cameron figured. The man seated before him, legs spread, unashamed at playing with his dick, was one half of the former most famous team of the brief golden days of professional beach volleyball. A ticket to the new American Beach Volleyball Federation. A means not to an end but to a beginning... if he agreed to take Troy on.

Cameron enjoyed this part of the game almost as much as the physical action on the beach. Always had, dating back to his days with Hutch. Heat flared in the head of his dick, unleashing concentric ripples through the rest of his body that were curiously icy in nature.

"Not convinced. Let me do something about that," Troy said and dropped to his knees.

"Ten years ago," Cameron said, grunting as Troy wrapped his grin around the head of his dick, "me and Hutch... we were on top of the world. We fucking owned the planet, every summer... *fuck,* that feels great. You done this before? Sucked dick?"

Troy regurgitated Cameron's cock. "I've had some practice, yeah."

"Keep working on your game, dude," Cameron ordered.

Troy resumed sucking and toyed with Cameron's nuts for added effect—clearly appreciated, judging by the other man's happy grunts.

"If the old league hadn't gone belly-up, fuck... yeah, work my dick as far down as you can. Don't just suck the fucker, make love to it with your face. Fucking league president mismanaged funds. Me and Hutch, we were close... too close..."

Troy lapped at Cameron's balls before moving behind them, stealing his first taste of asshole.

"The end of the ABVF was the end of us," Cameron continued.

He drew Troy up from the floor, fumbled the other man's shorts off his butt and down to his hairy ankles, taking the boxer-briefs beneath with them. Then Cameron leaned forward and pressed his nostrils against Troy's ball sac—considerably hairier than his shaved set. "Nice."

"They're so fucking ripe, I can smell them from here," Troy chuckled.

Cameron licked his lips. "I like what I smell. What I see."

"Enough to make it official? You and me, partnered up against the rest of the competition on Los Hombres?"

"Maybe," Cameron said. For the next ten or so minutes, the only conversation passed in happy groans.

"A great opportunity," Cameron huffed between sips of air. "The new league's well-funded. With Hutch's and my history... former partners turned archrivals... man, it's *money.*"

Troy drew back, slammed in again. Only his balls stopped him from fucking Cameron deeper. "And you need a new right-hand man. A Dude Friday."

"What I need," Cameron said, bent over with the younger man's damp flesh atop his, "is a partner who knows the game. More than that, who knows his place in the game—on and off the sand court."

He pulled back, so that just the head of his dick and an inch or so of shaft remained lodged in Cameron's hole, only to ram his cock in fully, right to the bush and balls. "You know what a solid teammate I am. I'm great, man," Troy answered through clenched teeth.

"You sure the fuck are," Cameron said. "Now fuck me. Oh yeah, *fuck my shit, bro!*"

Troy did as ordered.

* * *

"But I need you to understand how this works. You may have fucked me and fucked me better than most. All, in fact, except for the way Hutch used to."

Sitting naked, his hairy athlete's legs and big feet spread, his balls puddling beneath a swollen dick that hadn't fully softened even after its second nutting, Troy offered a high-five.

Cameron met it, the thunderclap of their hands almost as electric, as intimate, as mouths had been to cocks, cocks to assholes; almost as arousing as the mouth to asshole and the kiss that followed.

"Pick me," Troy said while scratching at his nuts, toying with his cock, nowhere near spent. "I'll fuck you every day, as often as you want."

"You may fuck me," Cameron said, all business, "but you're the beta dawg everywhere else. I'm the alpha. I'm on top. I tell you when to bust your load and how hard."

Troy waved the same fingers he'd used to ogle his meat, dismissing the conditions as a minor concession. "Whatever you say, dude. *Sir.*"

Cameron smiled. "That's more like it."

"So it's a done deal?"

Cameron maneuvered back between Troy's legs. "We're not done yet."

Troy sighed, "Yeah, suck my dick, sir."

"I'm gonna suck it and then you're going to fuck me again, and when we hit Los Hombres for the ABVF tryouts, we're gonna fuck Hutch and his new pretty-boy partner. Fuck 'em badly."

"I like what I'm hearing," Troy said, a cocky smirk forming on his mouth.

"First, Los Hombres. Then in the weeks ahead, we'll fuck

them again on Myrtle Beach, on Daytona, on Blacks and Long and Malibu and every other stop on the tour."

Hutch stood on the sand, no longer a man of thirty-five but in his twenties again. He gazed through the net at their opponents, a cocky dude named Troy, some flashy stallion with a goatee and a bit of Olympic gold on his resume, and a familiar face— one he'd seen often between his legs or underneath his as he'd fucked the dude's ass in that other life and time. Cameron had aged well. Suddenly, Hutch was thirty-five again, and it was Rio standing beside him, his partner in a sport he loved—despite it so often breaking his heart.

The two sides faced off. Music from the loudspeakers and excited chatter from the crowd rose, shorting out in a crackle, becoming a dull, distant whine.

Rio assumed the sharp angle to cover the seam. Hutch took the blocker position to cover the power angle.

Coin toss. Opening tip.

The big white ball tumbled out of the sky. Hutch tensed, smiled. His hearing returned, that old cacophony like the music of a favorite, almost-forgotten tune that suddenly belts out of the radio, transporting the listener through time.

And then he was flying off his feet again, carried on the summer breeze, the sweat pouring and the sunlight narcotic.

Side out.

SAND DREAMS

Jay Starre

The sun rose behind Blake to cast its shimmering light on the rolling surf as it danced rhythmically against the beach. At the break of dawn the waves had been strong enough for him to ride, but had tamed themselves after his first hour of gliding pleasure.

His board lay beside him. The beach just south of Monterey was deserted, except for a lone sunbather on his blanket. The blond dude pretended to read a book but glanced over at the tall, lean surfer with obvious interest more often than he perused the pages of his book.

Blake pretended not to notice Colby as he gazed out to sea. His toes stroked the sand under his bare feet in unconscious mimicry of the softly beating waves a few yards below. He loved the sand most of all about beaches. He didn't really like getting it in his trunks and around his balls and the crack of his ass, but he did like to feel it between his toes and under the bare soles of his feet, like now. He loved just to lie in it on a sunny day and enjoy the sensual feel of it along his calves, his bare back, his shoulders, and his arms. He liked wet sand, sometimes cool and sometimes steamy warm.

Sometimes he even dreamed about sand. His mind wandered as the surge and ebb of the gently beating waves calmed and mesmerized him. He realized he had spent a great deal of his life on the sand. As much as possible, actually.

He glanced back at Colby on his blanket and smiled, reminded of where his love affair with sand had truly begun.

A decade ago, when he was just twenty and a lifeguard on Hermosa Beach, he had fallen for a muscular blond roller-blader. Every day as he patrolled the busy Los Angeles area beach, he'd spot that bright platinum head as its owner bladed past. He began having cock-stirring fantasies about the jock from the first time he laid eyes on him.

Blake was a surf bum when he wasn't doing his lifeguard thing for cash. With shaggy auburn hair, a deep tan, bright blue eyes, and a wide, pleasant face, he was used to being noticed. He rarely had to seek out any other hot dudes for friendship— or fun and games. They came to him. It took less than a week for the blader to take notice and make his move.

Colby rolled up to him and spun to an expert halt. A brilliant smile in a freckled face, a few words of fairly inane chat, and then the dude was abruptly coming on to him. "I'm going up north on Saturday to Humboldt County for a week of camping on the beach. Want to come along? We could have some serious fun, I bet."

The soft green eyes sparkled and the smile teased. But he meant what he said. Blake's stiffening cock urged him to agree to the impromptu offer. He knew he could get the time off if he wanted to.

"Sounds like an awesome plan. You got wheels? I'd want to bring my board."

"No problem. I've got a pickup. So Saturday it is."

Blake had never been to the beaches in Northern California. Buddies told him the surf could be good, but the water was cold and the air didn't get as warm as it did in Southern California. None of that really mattered to him. It was an adventure. And as a bonus, he was pretty sure he'd get a chance to get naked with the blond roller-blader.

They hit it off right away. Colby was a chatterbox and Blake was a good listener. It took all day to drive the hundreds of miles north to Humboldt County, but the time flew by. Colby was a sophomore majoring in natural history; he commented nonstop on the spectacular scenery as they traveled through the hot Central Valley, then the rolling hills of the wine country, and finally arrived at the rugged Humboldt coast.

His friends had been right. The beaches of Humboldt County were nothing like Southern California beaches. First off, stunning redwood forests hugged the shore above the coastal cliffs, an easy drive from their camping spot on the beach. They hiked through the ancient woods almost every day. He felt dwarfed by the soaring trees and their gigantic girth.

And there was the fog—every damn morning. It swirled in off the cool water and insinuated itself nearly everywhere. That was usually when they went for their hikes in the redwoods. Shrouded in the mist, the trees quietly endured, century after century.

There were some things about the fog Blake discovered could be a bonus. They awoke their first morning together huddled side by side in their small tent. He crawled out of his sleeping bag to peer out the tent door and discovered the thick blanket coating everything. He couldn't help a groan of dismay.

Awakened by his new friend's movement and groan, Colby laughed and turned Blake's groan to yelping glee, sliding a hand between the surfer's thighs from behind and cupping his dangling nads.

"My, my, what big balls you have! I like that. Can I suck on them? That might brighten up a foggy morning for you."

Hoping for some action but not yet ready to push it, Blake had slept naked the night before on purpose. But all they'd done was talk. He'd fallen fast asleep to the sound of Colby's deep voice chattering on and on.

Now, with the big dude's hand on his nads, it was obvious he was about to get some of that action. "Hell yeah! And you can suck my dick after that."

Blake scooted backwards and raised a knee to settle over Colby's grinning face. His fat balls plopped right down on the freckled nose and plump lips. His cock stiffened up nicely as lips opened wide and sucked in his balls.

Moaning with pleasure, he spread his legs wide and began to hump that wet mouth. At the same time, he yanked down the zipper on Colby's sleeping bag and tore it open. Right away, the muscular blond's cock reared up, bright pink and twitching. It was thick, with a huge knob at the head. Blake dropped down to take that blunt head whole.

The turgid meat pulsed in his mouth. Colby shoved up with his hips to fuck wildly while he slurped loudly over Blake's nads. His big hands seized the surfer's naked butt and kneaded it as his tongue and lips massaged his balls.

Blake gripped his hefty thighs and spread them. Below the cock and balls, Colby's ivory-pale flesh was dotted with a few more freckles. A pink hole pouted in the smooth crack he'd opened up. He sucked on that huge boner while gazing down at the hole and contemplating what he'd like to do to it.

Fingers roamed into Blake's crack and found his hole. They boldly stroked and tickled the snug ass-lips as Blake grunted and wriggled against them. The mouth surrounding his ball sac drooled all over his crotch. He dropped lower over Colby's cock to suck in half the throbbing shaft.

As those fingers continued to tickle his sensitive butt-rim, he tried some of the same on the blond's pink asshole. He pushed back on Colby's big hamstrings with his elbows and held them high and wide apart before he began to run his hands all over the pale cheeks and crack. The hole pushed outward against his rubbing fingertips as he began to play with it.

Colby spit out Blake's fat balls and immediately gobbled up his cock. With his head rolling backwards, his throat opened up and he accepted the tapered head deep in his gullet.

Both gurgling over cock, they rubbed each other's assholes and squirmed around on the sleeping bag on its pliant bed of sand. Neither probed past the distended, quivering lips, but both swallowed cock right down to the balls.

It didn't last. Colby's big body heaved beneath Blake as he rammed his cock as deep as possible into the surfer's wet mouth and squirmed around the fingers stroking his asshole. He rubbed his own fingers all over Blake's pouting butt-lips as he deep-throated his cock with snorts and gurgles.

They shot. First it was Blake, but Colby joined him only a moment later. The surfer rose up off Colby's sucking mouth and sprayed his chin and lips, while Blake clamped his own mouth over the blond's plump knob and sucked him dry.

Blake rolled off with a satisfied moan and turned around to face Colby. "I don't mind a little fog if we can still find something fun like this to do."

With a wink and a satisfied smirk, Colby agreed. "Hell yeah. I'm definitely looking forward to more of the same. Much more."

There was more about the fog he liked. It was cool, a bonus

when the rest of California sweltered in ninety-degree summer heat. It made everything look cozy and mysterious. It made it seem as if they were alone in the world.

Fortunately, it lifted every day after lunch. The warm sunlight seemed even more dazzling in contrast to the drab gray it replaced. He surfed then, while Colby combed the beach for starfish and shells and all the natural crap he was so keen to investigate.

Paddling out to set up for some waves, Blake turned to face the shore and caught sight of the crouching blond busily probing the nooks and crannies of the jumbled boulders a little north of their campsite. In a pair of jean cutoffs and nothing else, his powerful body gleamed with a freckled flush in the sparkling sunshine.

He grinned as he thought how lucky they were. He loved to surf and Colby didn't, but they both loved the beach. He had to admit he was sometimes a loner, and surfing allowed him the luxury of being alone with only the sea and the shore and his thoughts. Colby was definitely more sociable and loved to chatter his ear off, but he seemed quite capable of keeping himself occupied.

The beach was so totally different than what he was used to. The redwood forest loomed on cliffs above, instead of the layers of beach houses and apartments that rose from the Southern California beaches. There was really no one around either, unlike the bustling crowds and honking cars of LA.

He caught a sweet wave and rode it in. Nothing spectacular, but that suited him. He preferred the smooth effortless glide rather than the wild danger of crashing pipelines. Just being a part of the wave, balancing on his board, smelling the salty air, and tasting the salty sea were all the thrill he needed—at least as far as surfing was concerned.

It was their second afternoon when Colby offered Blake the thrill he really wanted. He had just come in from an hour of surfing. Traipsing up through the warmed-up sand, he deposited his board beside their tent and looked around for his blond buddy.

"Over here. I've been watching you. All that tan muscle balanced on that board. Hot. Really hot. Really, really hot."

Blake's mouth dropped open. On the other side of the tent, in a little patch of sand between their camp and the fern-covered wall of the cliff behind it, Colby awaited him. His cutoffs were beside him. He knelt on all fours in the sand, his head craned around to face Blake as he wriggled his naked ass and winked.

"Goddamn," Blake hissed as he raced forward to cover the few yards that separated them.

"It's all yours. You can eat it, you can finger it, or you can fuck it. Or all three."

"All three," Blake grunted out as he dropped to his knees between the blond's spread thighs.

With trembling hands, he seized the hefty ass cheeks and pulled them wide apart. The hole he'd teased the previous morning pouted open. In the bright sunlight it flushed pale pink. He groaned aloud as he dove down to clamp his mouth over it.

"Fuck yeah! Show me how a surf bum can use his tongue. Ohh yeah. Get me ready for that juicy cock of yours. That's it! Lick it, Blake!"

Colby wasn't about to keep his mouth shut, and Blake choked back laughter as he sucked and licked at the tight hole while pulling Colby's cheeks as wide open as possible. The hole gaped open in response to his slurps. He buried his tongue between the convulsing lips.

He ate Colby out while the muscular blond wriggled enthusiastically and egged him on with a constant barrage of nasty encouragement. Blake was glad they were out of sight and earshot of anyone who might be passing by on the beach below.

Licking and tonguing were soon not enough. He got his fingers in there and began to probe as he licked. Spit coated the lips and eased the way for an index finger to slither into the snug cavern beyond.

"Yeah! Bury that finger in my ass. Twist it around. Like that. Deeper! I fucking love it!"

Spitting as he lapped at the hole with his tongue, he crammed his finger in past the second knuckle, found the prostate, and rubbed it. He pulled part of the way out and then thrust back in. He spit some more and gently added another finger.

Colby's sphincter resisted slightly, then yawned open. He grunted and heaved backwards to swallow up both fingers while crying out for more. The snug feel of palpitating ass-lips clamping and massaging his fingers had Blake wanting more, too.

Colby apparently felt the same. "I put some lube in my shorts. Get it out and use it. I need some cock. And I'm betting your cock wants some of this ass!"

Blake didn't mind obeying the demanding bottom's nasty orders. He actually liked it. There was no guessing involved— and no worries about doing the wrong thing. He rose from his feast with a smack of his lips. He gazed at his handiwork while he reached out with his right hand to rummage in Colby's discarded shorts lying in the sand beside them.

Two fingers of his right hand were still digging around in the flushed hole, and his hand protruded from the ivory ass crack. His smooth butt cheeks rose up from Colby's narrow waist like mountains. He was shorter than the tall surfer but must have outweighed him by a good fifty pounds, all of it muscle.

Blake found the tube of lubricant and flipped off the lid with his fingertips. Upending it over that heaving butt, he squirted.

A huge stream of the clear gel splattered that can and slithered down between the pale mounds. He squirted a little more, just to be sure. Blake firmly believed that you could never use too much lube.

The goo ran down around his buried fingers. He pumped it into the seething hole, stretching the sphincter out so that his cock could replace his fingers. He took his time feeding Colby the lube, even though he continued to demand cock *right now.*

"Hold on, Colby. I gotta loosen you up. And I have to get my pants off," he finally blurted out.

"Well, get those shorts off, then! I'm dying for a good hard fuck. Can't you tell? I knew from the moment we met that you'd be into my ass. I just knew it! Now get that cock up my butt."

He wriggled his hefty butt to emphasize the point but laughed at the same time. He knew how he sounded, and it didn't bother him. Blake liked him even more for that.

He had to abandon the steamy hole momentarily in order to get out of his flowery surf shorts. His fingers eased from the quivering slot with a slurp, followed by a stream of lube. He'd packed a lot of it in there.

Transfixed by that oozing hole and big white butt, he scrambled to crawl out of his shorts and kick them aside. His cock bobbed out between them as he re-positioned himself between Colby's knees and closer to his rearing can.

He leaned in to rub his stiff rod between the parted cheeks. It looked dark and menacing against the ivory ass. He hoped like hell it wasn't going to hurt Colby when he buried it up his butt. Squirming eagerly back against his rubbing cock and demanding to get fucked, Colby seemed willing to take it no matter what.

"Here it comes, buddy. Cock, like you wanted. Tell me if it hurts," he warned.

He planted the tapered head in place and began to push. His fingers had done a good job of stretching out the sphincter, and Colby's wriggling along with all that lube helped too. His cock-head disappeared. Clamping ass-lips pulled him deeper. He grunted and shoved.

"Hell! You're killing me with that gigantic dick! You bastard!"

Colby's laughter was followed by a mighty heave of those huge ass cheeks. He gulped up nearly all of Blake's boner.

"Oh my god. Oh my god," Blake moaned.

They fucked. With Colby rearing and humping Blake's cock like it was the best thing he'd ever had up his hungry ass, there was no reason for the auburn-haired surfer to hold back. He rammed in and out, balls-deep. His lean hips slapped mercilessly against Colby's big solid ass-cheeks.

The warm, fog-dampened sand beneath Blake's knees and shins created a soft and yielding bed. He was acutely aware of the sensual feel of it, and that Colby knelt in it too, his own knees and shins and toes burrowing into it. They were totally naked, the sunlight and the sand and the sounds of the surf below surrounding them. It was the first time he'd ever had sex outdoors, and he would never forget it.

He reached around Colby's waist and pumped his plump cock with a slippery hand. The big university student slid his knees even wider apart in the sand and cried out for more. Blake pumped and fucked relentlessly as the sun bathed them from above and they grew sweatier and sweatier.

The sensation of that sweet hole clinging, then releasing, then swallowing him up again pushed him to the brink, but he held back. Colby seemed poised at the same precipice. He hollered and swore and begged and heaved. His cock grew so stiff it seemed as if it was about to burst in Blake's pumping hand. It

finally did. Cum erupted as the hefty blond blew his load. Blake
followed with a dizzying spew of his own.

The remainder of that week was just as exciting. They sucked
and fucked day and night, in the fog, in the sunlight, in the tent,
in the surf. Colby wasn't afraid to experiment, and Blake was
happy to oblige.

Ten years later, as he recalled that awesome week, Blake
realized that his time with Colby had affected him in many
unexpected ways. He'd grown more adventurous and traveled
to beaches all over the world.

In Hawaii he watched a surf competition on Oahu where the
waves were so high and daunting he was absolutely terrified. At
Bondi Beach in Australia he watched a lifeguard competition
where the lifeguards unexpectedly pulled their skimpy suits into
the cracks of their asses when they boarded their surf canoes.
He could practically see their entire butts, right there in the
bright Australian sunlight.

In Rio the slums marched down to the beach and gangs
mingled with tourists. He met a hot Brazilian thug who wanted
to become an American porn star. His dick was cannon-sized
and he knew how to use it, so Blake told him quite honestly
he had a good chance at that. In the Yucatán the water was
a beautiful azure and the sand sparkling white. Mayan ruins
rose right up from the beach where he fucked a Mexican tour
guide behind some rocks with the surf splashing against their
feet. On the sun-washed beaches of South Africa, he spotted sea
lions and whales while riding the surf. Water buffalo and zebras
grazed on grass above the sandy shore.

But here he was back in California again. Home.

He turned away from the water and faced the cliffs. No one
was around, except of course Colby, still pretending to read on
a blanket. He'd been watching Blake while he surfed, and was

watching him now out of the corner of his eyes.

He left his board where it was and strode over to the quiet figure.

"You've been watching me pretty close. I think you want some of this."

He pulled out his cock and shoved it into the gawking sunbather's mouth before he could even speak. He fucked that mouth good and deep, grinning down at the wide green eyes and freckled nose before he finally relented and pulled out with a nasty slurp.

Colby pushed him away, but only so he could tear off his shorts and drop down onto the sand beside his blanket, white ass rearing.

"And I think you want some of this," Colby teased, wagging his powerful ass.

In the sand, just like that first fuck ten years earlier. Blake crawled in behind his boyfriend and knelt in the sand between his spread thighs. Now it was time to satisfy his adventurous yearnings with the one person who knew him best.

His sand dreams had found a home.

SUMMER FOLK

Michael Bracken

W e went to the beach every summer whether we wanted to or not, and we stayed in a six-bedroom beach house with an ever-changing number of relatives. The boys shared one bedroom, the girls shared another, and our parents paired off into the other four bedrooms. The general overseer for the summer—my grandmother, all the years I was growing up— had an efficiency apartment above the two-car garage. Our extended family lived in the house from Memorial Day weekend until Labor Day weekend, and when and how long each family stayed depended on a variety of factors, often involving available vacation time and who had insulted whom over the Christmas holidays.

When I was young, I enjoyed spending several weeks at the beach with my cousins. As a teenager I resented mandatory fun in the sun when what I most craved was to lock myself in my bedroom, smoke pot, and fantasize about some of the guys in my gym class. During college, I skipped summers at the beach because I was working or enrolled in summer classes, but I had no job prospects when I graduated as an English major in the middle of a recession. My mother convinced me to spend the entire summer at the house to act as general overseer, a responsibility my grandmother had tired of and no other relative had stepped forward to accept.

My duties were minimal: manage the summer finances, keep the fridge stocked with staples, ensure that we never ran out of toilet paper, and call the appropriate repairman if the plumbing stopped up or one of the children threw a baseball through the front window. In exchange, I would live rent-free in the efficiency apartment above the garage for more than three months while I continued my job search by applying for positions I found online.

The house was empty when I arrived the Thursday preceding Memorial Day weekend. I walked through the place with the caretaker, a local man who lived in town and took care of the property three seasons out of four. Charlie had already uncovered all the furniture, washed all the windows, and otherwise prepared the house for my family's arrival. I had not seen him in several years and was surprised at how slowly he moved and how much trouble he had climbing the stairs to the second floor. After I saw that everything was in order, I followed Charlie's rattletrap pickup truck a mile north into town to stock up on the things we needed to start the summer.

I had a shopping list handed down by my grandmother; purchasing everything on the list filled two carts. A woman as old as the town rang up my purchases and an attractive blond man near my age bagged everything. He wore tight-fitting jeans and a torso-hugging polo shirt with the store's logo embroidered on one side of his chest and a name badge reading "Tony" pinned to the other. He bagged quickly and efficiently, hesitating every fifth item or so to brush a wayward lock of blond hair away from his pale blue eyes.

"Need help getting all this out?" he asked.

I did and I told him so.

As we pushed the carts out of the store, Tony said, "Looks like you're preparing for an invasion."

I laughed. "My family has a summer house south of town. I'm the advance guard."

"You're summer folk?"

"Most of my life," I said as we loaded everything into my car. "Haven't made it the past few years, though."

He looked me up and down as if taking my measure as a man, but I couldn't tell from his expression what his assessment might be. Then we both reached for my car's trunk to close it and his hand covered mine. An electric tingle shot up my arm, coursed through my entire body, and caused a tightening in my crotch. I took a deep breath. "Bag boy" wasn't on my grandmother's shopping list so, no matter how appealing I found Tony, he was a seductive treat best left at the grocery store. I said, "I have to go."

We closed the trunk together and Tony stepped away.

There wasn't much else to say, so I climbed behind the wheel of my Mustang and watched Tony's jeans-clad ass as he wheeled the two carts back into the store.

I saw Tony jogging along the beach early the next morning. He wore neon-blue running shorts, white running shoes covered with clinging wet sand, and nothing else, revealing the long, lean body of a swimmer. Even though it was an unusually warm May morning on the Jersey shore, it was too cold for me to be outside without my full-length terry-cloth robe wrapped around me. I was sitting on the deck of the main house drinking coffee, enjoying my last morning of solitude before my relatives invaded. Tony saw me watching him and waved.

I called to him. "I have a fresh pot of coffee and a spare cup. You interested?"

He crossed the beach and climbed the steps. By the time he reached the deck, I had ducked into the house, retrieved a cup, and was filling it with coffee from the thermal carafe. As he settled into the deck chair next to me, his pebbled skin, tight areolas, and firm nipples revealed that he was colder than he let on—he probably needed the coffee. I asked, "Cream? Sugar?"

"Black's fine."

I handed him the cup and he sipped from it. Then he glanced over his shoulder at the house. "This your place?"

The house had been in my family for several generations, owned and maintained by a family trust overseen by a board of directors elected by and made up of family members. I said, "It's as much mine as anyone else's."

He brushed a long lock of blond hair away from his eyes. "Must be nice."

"How's that?"

"To have a place like this to spend your summers," he said. "I've lived down the shore my entire life, but never in a place like this."

Tony and I had probably crossed paths when we were younger, but we never would have played together. Children of the locals and the summer folk intermingled only by accident. Now that we were older, our differences seemed less significant and the vibe I felt from his proximity suggested we had more in common than expected. For a moment I imagined what it might be like to lick the sweat off his chest, drum my fingers on his abdominal six-pack, or rest my hand on his muscular thigh before intermingling with him. My thoughts made my robe tent beneath the table and I leaned forward.

Just as I convinced myself to place my hand on Tony's forearm to see his reaction, he finished his coffee and placed the empty cup on the serving tray next to the carafe. As he stood, he said, "Thanks for this."

"Any time," I told him. "You're welcome any time."

His gaze wandered over me, taking in my tousled bed hair and tightly fastened robe. "If you're ever in town some evening," he said, "come by the Dew Drop Inn. I usually stop there after work."

"I will," I promised, though I wasn't yet certain it was a promise I would keep.

He took the steps two at a time down to the beach and continued jogging south, away from town. I watched him until I ran out of coffee. By then he was barely a speck in the distance.

My relatives started arriving early that evening, beginning with my mother's oldest brother and his second wife. By the time the sun set Saturday evening, the house was filled with family members, including my parents and grandmother, representing all generations and various degrees of separation. The house was ready for their arrival, but I wasn't. I had forgotten how loud a houseful of my relatives could be, and I was glad to disappear into the garage apartment each evening.

Memorial Day meant hot dogs grilled on the beach, tubs of potato salad, and pots of baked beans. The children drank gallons of pop and the adults worked their way through several bottles of wine and a few cases of beer, some starting as early as breakfast with mimosas on the deck. By the time the sun went down the questions began.

Most of them hadn't seen me in four years and wanted to

know everything about my life. I answered the questions I could, deflected the questions I didn't wish to answer, and did my best to avoid the nosiest among them.

By Wednesday I'd had enough of my relatives; even my private apartment over the garage was too close to them. I drove up the coast to town and found the Dew Drop Inn, a waterfront watering hole that catered to locals. I saw more plaid wool shirts than polo shirts and more work boots than penny loafers, so I knew as I crossed to the bar that I didn't fit in. I knew enough to order a beer rather than a mixed drink, and I carried my bottle to an empty booth where I could sit and watch the door.

I'd been there about twenty minutes and was well into my second beer before Tony arrived. He wore his work clothes but had removed his name badge. He ordered a beer and came to my table.

"Slumming?" he asked as he slid into the booth opposite me.

"Avoiding my family," I explained. "My grandmother wants to know when I'm planning to settle down with a nice girl and my mother wants to know when she'll have grandchildren."

He hesitated with his beer halfway to his lips. "You haven't told them?"

"Not yet."

"So summer folk have the same problems as the rest of us?"

I knew at that moment that we were speaking the same coded language. "You haven't told your family, either?"

"Nope." He lifted the beer the rest of the way to his lips and drained half the bottle.

I glanced around the bar and wondered what he did for companionship in a town small enough that everyone likely knew everyone else's business. I had finished my second beer by then and he had almost finished his first. I asked, "You want another?"

"Let's get out of here," he suggested. "I have beer in the fridge at home."

Home turned out to be a cottage on the inland side of town. We both parked in the driveway because a Jet Ski occupied the one-car garage; I had to step around a pair of body boards on the porch to reach the back door.

"Spend a lot of time in the water?" I asked as Tony pushed open the door and led me into the kitchen.

"On it, in it, or near it," he said.

The kitchen had been completely renovated, and Tony pulled two bottles of beer from the stainless-steel refrigerator. He opened both and handed one to me.

I put my bottle on the granite counter. "This isn't why we're here, is it?"

He shook his head and placed his beer next to mine, sweat from the bottles dripping onto the countertop. Months had passed since my last sexual encounter, and I had never been with a man I knew so little about.

Nervous, I pushed blond hair away from his blue eyes and then covered his lips with mine. Our kiss was long and deep and we were tugging at each other's clothes long before it ended.

After I peeled off his shirt, I kissed my way down his neck to his deeply tanned, hairless chest, pausing to suckle each of his nipples before dropping to my knees and unfastening his jeans. As I pulled his jeans and his boxers to his knees and let them drop to his ankles, Tony's thick cock sprang free of the confining material.

His cock was as pale as the rest of his skin from his waist to his thighs, evidence that he spent a good deal of time in nothing but running shorts and swimming trunks, and it throbbed in front of my face. I wrapped my fist around the base of his shaft and licked away a glistening drop of precum before I took the spongy soft helmet head in my mouth. As I licked his cock head, I pistoned my fist up and down the stiff shaft.

Tony held the back of my head, applying pressure that let me know he wanted me to take in more of his cock. I had not had a cock in my mouth since the New Year's Eve party at my frat house, so I took it in slowly, licking and sucking and licking more as it filled my oral cavity.

When I had taken in as much as I could, I pulled back and then did it again. I cupped Tony's sac with my free hand, massaging his balls as I stroked the delicate area between his sac and his ass with the tip of one finger.

Apparently I was moving too slow for Tony. As he held my head, he drew back his hips and pushed forward, driving his cock in and out of my mouth until he could restrain himself no longer. With one last thrust, he came, firing a thick wad of hot spunk against the back of my throat.

I didn't swallow because I never swallow. When his cock quit spasming, I stood and kissed Tony again, surprising him with a mouthful of his own cum. He pushed me away, spit into the sink, and quickly rinsed his mouth with a swallow of beer.

"That was a surprise," Tony said. "Nobody around here does that."

He pulled off his shoes and stepped out of his jeans and boxers. He helped me out of my clothes and then bent me over the island. I grabbed the granite countertop as he spread my legs and stepped between them. He dribbled olive oil down my ass crack until it dripped from my ball sac and then slid his middle finger down my crack until it was slick with olive oil.

He pressed the tip of his slickened finger against my asshole until my sphincter opened to admit it. His erection had returned and a moment later he pulled his finger free and replaced it with his cockhead. Then he grabbed my hips and pushed his entire length deep inside me.

My own cock was hard and I wrapped my fist around it. As Tony pounded into me from behind, I stroked my cock. The faster he pumped, the faster I pumped.

I came first, firing my load against the underside of the granite countertop, but Tony continued pounding into me for another dozen strokes until he couldn't restrain himself and he came with one final, powerful thrust.

He stood behind me, holding my hips as his cock throbbed inside my ass. He asked, "You have a name?"

"Chad."

After he pulled away, we dressed and drank our beers.

Then I left, wondering all the way back to my family's beach house if I had been too easy and if I would see Tony again.

But that wasn't the end of things. On the mornings when I woke early enough and took my coffee on the deck I would see Tony jogging south along the beach. Most mornings he wore gray sweats, no longer seeking to seduce me with his toned body. We waved, but he never approached while my family was present.

On those evenings when I tired of the never-ending parade of noisy relatives who moved in and out of the beach house during the summer, I drove myself to the Dew Drop Inn, shared a beer with Tony, and then followed him to his cottage.

By mid-July we stopped all pretense of running into one another at the inn: I drove directly to his place on those evenings when I tired of my extended family and desired his physical attention. We spent hours in Tony's bed. He taught me the value of a steady relationship, something I'd never really had in college. On his days off from the grocery store, Tony took me out on his Jet Ski or taught me how to body board at the beach north of town.

By the time our summer romance was half over, it was obvious neither of us wanted it to end—yet neither of us would broach the subject directly. We were trying to milk every moment of passion we could from our remaining time together.

"Summer folk always leave," Tony said one night as I was dressing to return to my family's beach house. He lay on his bed, still naked and sweaty from our earlier entanglement.

I pulled my shirt into place and tucked it into my chinos. "What if they didn't?"

"I've lived here my entire life, Chad. Summer folk always leave. That's just the way it is." He turned away, unwilling to hear me deny the truth we both knew.

One afternoon near the end of August, our caretaker's wife called to tell us that Charlie had suffered a heart attack and was in the hospital.

"It doesn't look good," she said. "Even if he survives this, he won't be able to continue working."

My grandmother led a troop of older family members—those who had known Charlie for several decades—to the hospital. When they returned, my grandmother chaired a meeting of the family members present at the beach house and updated us all on his status. Labor Day weekend was rapidly approaching and we had limited time to find a replacement.

After more than an hour of discussion, I said, "I'll do it."

Every adult in the room turned to look at me. No member of the family had ever served as caretaker for the beach house, just as no member of the family had ever lived year-round on the property.

"You'll have to commit to the entire year," my grandmother said.

I knew what Charlie had been paid. It wasn't much, but

combined with rent-free living in the garage apartment, I could scrape by. I could maybe find a part-time job in town for extra spending money or spend my time applying to graduate school. My only other option was to boomerang back to my bedroom in my parents' house because I hadn't done any online job hunting since the night I'd first met Tony at the Dew Drop Inn. I said, "That's not a problem."

The adults talked for another hour, came up with no better solution, and finally offered me the position.

The next night, while reclining on Tony's bed watching him undress, I told him I would be remaining at the beach house after Labor Day.

He turned. "How long?"

"At least until next summer." As he settled onto the bed next to me, I told him what had happened.

"This changes everything," Tony said when I finished.

"I know," I said. "Summer folk don't always leave."

He stared deep into my eyes, placed his hands on either side of my head, and kissed me—softly, tenderly, his lips lingering as if we had all the time in the world. Then he caressed me, letting his fingers explore every inch of my body before I turned my back to him. I handed him the nearly empty tube of lube from his nightstand and soon he entered me.

We made love—slow, sweet love, unlike all the times before, when our sex had been hard and fast and without commitment—and I fell asleep in Tony's arms.

For the first time since we'd met, I spent the night, slipping back into the garage apartment at the beach house moments before dawn. I'd barely been home five minutes when I heard someone climbing the steps.

I opened the apartment door just as my grandmother reached the little deck that served as a porch.

"You think nobody knows," she said, "but we do. Some of us. You be careful. Don't let this local boy break your heart."

I smiled. "I won't, Grandma. I'll be careful."

"And if he does, you let me know. I'm sure we can find someone to watch the house if you need to leave."

"I'll be okay."

She patted my arm. "So you clean up and then come over to the house. I'm fixing pancakes this morning and I need your help."

My relatives started heading home on Saturday, just as noisy in their departures as they were in their arrivals. The last to leave—a second cousin and her family—drove away mid-afternoon on Labor Day. The next morning I had the entire place to myself. I woke early, made coffee, and sat on the deck awaiting Tony's arrival.

Our summer romance was over. Now it was time to see what the future really held.

ABOUT THE AUTHORS

SHANE ALLISON's writings have graced the pages of dozens of journals and saucy anthologies; a poetry collection, *Slut Machine;* and a book-length poem/memoir, *I Remember.* He has edited more than a dozen gay erotica anthologies. He resides in Florida, where he is hard at work on his first novel.

MICHAEL BRACKEN's short fiction has been published in *Best Gay Romance 2010, Beautiful Boys, Biker Boys, Black Fire, Boy Fun, Boys Getting Ahead, Country Boys, Freshmen, The Handsome Prince, Homo Thugs, The Mammoth Book of Best New Erotica 4, Men, Muscle Men, Teammates,* and many other anthologies and periodicals.

H. L. CHAMPA has been published in numerous anthologies including *College Boys, The Handsome Prince, Afternoon Delight, Skater Boys* and *Hard Working Men.* Her short stories can be found at Dreamspinner Press, Ravenous Romance, and Torquere Press. Find more online at heidichampa.blogspot.com.

After years away from her writing, **RAVEN DE HART** again picked up her quill to craft saucy stories and tantalizing tales. When not writing, she can be found tending her gardens, drinking wine, or researching myth and history. More information can be found at dehartslist.blogspot.com.

Living in Portland, Oregon, **DAVID HOLLY** is fascinated by the human penchant for odd mythologies, bizarre rituals, diverse religions, forlorn hopes, and broken dreams. He is fond of strong coffee, red wine, English bitters, rich stout, nude beaches, and hot-looking guys. Find out more at facebook.com/david.holly2 and gaywriter.org.

D.K. JERNIGAN (JerniganWrites@gmail.com) loves men who love men, hard cider, and long walks on the beach. He lives in California with the most amazing husband in the world and a devoted German Shepherd and has been published in *Spellbinding: Tales from the Magic University* from Ravenous Romance.

GREGORY L. NORRIS lives and writes at the outer limits of New Hampshire. A former feature writer and columnist for *Sci Fi Magazine* who also worked on Paramount's *Star Trek: Voyager* series, his books include *The Q Guide to Buffy the Vampire Slayer* and *The Fierce and Unforgiving Muse*. Learn more at gregorylnorris.blogspot.com.

MISS PEACH is a former middle school, high school, and college writing teacher. An accomplished erotica writer published in such places as *Hustler Fantasies*, *Readerotica* volumes 2 and 3, Forthegirls.com, and vamperotic.com, she also creates custom erotic fiction for individuals. Ms. Peach lives in Massachusetts and plays a mean banjo.

ROB ROSEN, author of the critically acclaimed novels *Sparkle: The Queerest Book You'll Ever Love, Divas Las Vegas, Hot Lava,* and *Southern Fried,* has had short stories featured in more than 150 anthologies. Please visit him at www.therobrosen.com.

DOMINIC SANTI (dominicsanti@yahoo.com) is a former technical editor turned rogue whose stories have appeared in many dozens of publications, including *Hot Daddies, Caught Looking, Kink,* and several volumes of *Best Gay Erotica.* Future plans include more dirty short stories and an even dirtier historical novel.

JAY STARRE pumps out erotic fiction for gay men's magazines and more than four dozen anthologies, including *Surfer Boys, Skater Boys,* and *Model Men,* all from Cleis Press. He is the author of two novels, *The Erotic Tales of the Knights Templars* and *The Lusty Adventures of the Knossos Prince.*

TROY STORM crosses his genres in straight, bi, and gay romances, confessions, short stories, and novels published on the Internet and in print under various virtuoso pseudonyms. Two hundred or so, and still rolling.

EMILY VEINGLORY is a New Zealand–born writer of erotic romance, dark fantasy, and gay fiction. Her novels *Father of Dragons* and *Lovers of Ghosts* are available from Samhain Publishing. For more information see emilyveinglory.com.

LOGAN ZACHARY is a mystery author living in Minneapolis. His story collection *Calendar Boys* was published in 2012. His stories can be found in *Hard Hats, Taken by Force, Ride*

Me Cowboy, Surfer Boys, and *Boys Caught in the Act,* among others. He can be reached at loganzachary2002@yahoo.com.

ABOUT
THE EDITOR

NEIL S. PLAKCY is the author of nineteen novels and collections of short stories, as well as the editor of many anthologies for Cleis Press, including *Hard Hats, Surfer Boys, Skater Boys, The Handsome Prince, Model Men,* and *Sexy Sailors.* He began his erotic writing career with a story for *Honcho* magazine called "The Cop Who Caught Me," and he's been writing about cops and sex ever since, most recently with six books in the *Mahu* mystery series. He lives in South Florida, and his website is mahubooks.com.